For our lovely mums, who both gave us

the joy of laughter:

Annie Mary Fowler (1935-2022)

Alice Kathleen Warde (1926-2019)

Historic images courtesy of the British Library
https://www.flickr.com/photos/britishlibrary/

(which Tim thinks is probably the best rabbit hole to fall down on the entire internet)

Cover and other graphics designed by Tim Fowler.

Front cover photo of Rory Bremner by Steve Ullathorne.

All material © Tim & Mary Fowler 2025. All rights reserved.

Two Idiots and a Genius

Our Story of Writing for Rory

By

Mary & Tim Fowler

Foreword by

Rory Bremner

Comedy, we may say, is society protecting itself – with a smile

J.B Priestley

Fools are my theme, let satire be my song

Lord Byron

It is precisely against the darkness of the world that comedy arises, and it is best when that is not hidden.

JRR Tolkien

Foreword by Rory Bremner

It started with a tweet. I was doing a series of tour shows and would often send a general tweet out to the next town en route and ask for a bit of local info I could mention in my show. A particular favourite was Radlett. I tweeted 'what happens in Radlett?', and in came the first reply: 'Stays in Radlett'.

En route for Durham, I sent out an instruction along the lines of 'Durham, Friday. Activate the Plan'. A short while after, a tweet came back. A single word. '*ACTIVATED*' I smiled. have an agent in Durham, I thought. A sleeper cell, waiting quietly for the call to action.

And so it proved. Amused by the reply, I direct-messaged the sender and the day after the show, Agent Fowler arrived at my hotel. A tall, bespectacled man in a wheelchair with long hair, a ready smile and a great sense of humour. 'The name's Fowler. Tim Fowler' he might have said but didn't. By day he was a librarian at Durham University. By night, he devoured comedy, particularly satire, and had followed my Channel Four shows with John Bird and John Fortune for many years. We talked, enjoyed each other's company, and soon after I asked if he fancied writing some lines for my shows. The plan was ACTIVATED.

Not long after my meeting with Agent Tim, a second agent surfaced. Tim's soon to be wife, Mary. Herself recruited with a one-word tweet, sent by Tim in one of his darker moments when life was getting the better of him. 'Struggling' he wrote. Out of the blue, Mary replied. 'Is that a baby struggle?'. A play on words worthy of the Uxbridge English Dictionary on *I'm Sorry I Haven't A Clue,* Radio 4's antidote to panel games, where the panel make up new definitions for words. (e.g.: Tadpole: ever so slightly Polish. Acoustic: A Scottish cattle prod. Sanctity: Five French Breasts. You get the gist).

And so, the two agents became one. A team of writers whose shared sense of humour and way of looking at the world could now be turned into material to be performed.

I was always on the look-out for new writers who could supplement and inspire my own routines. I learnt from the best: John Bird and John Fortune, together with my life-long writing partner, John Langdon. Bird and Fortune were themselves veterans of the 1960s satire 'boom' and their routines on *Bremner, Bird and Fortune, [where a hapless minister, general, spokesman or captain of industry would be interviewed, laying bare their complacency or incompetence,]* are timeless gems of satire.

Satire, in its original sense, is not necessarily funny. It can be a dark, angry, heavily ironic response to injustice, [as in Jonathan Swift's *Modest Proposal* of 1729, where the writer proposed that the starving poor in Ireland might alleviate their poverty by selling their children as food for the elite.] Nowadays, as part of light entertainment, what we call satire might simply be called topical comedy; needing, for TV, to be funny and entertaining, it's more ironic, playful, aiming for laughs rather than anger. *[Since the 60s and' That Was The Week That Was' it's become part of a British tradition of laughing at those in power rather than holding them to scorn. John Bird and Barry Humphries (aka Dame Edna) later regretted that everyone was becoming a comedian, everything was a frivolous send-up and Britain would, in Peter Cook's words, end up 'sinking giggling into the sea'.*

Into this world of frivolity come agents Tim and Mary, instinctively understanding the art of topical comedy- being topical and satirical while not forgetting to be funny. I always think of it as two lines: a comedy line and a true line- one funny, one factual- and when the two come together, preferably voiced by a funny character, something is created: the audience laugh while recognising the truth of what's being said. Thus David Cameron: "People asked me when I became Prime Minister, do I want to make the rich richer, or do I want to make the poor poorer? I think we've managed to do both."

It usually means trying to make sense of things before you make nonsense of them. Often Bird, Fortune and I would spend hours trying to tease out what the government or opposition were up to and understand a policy, while the politicians were thinking up jokes for Prime Minister's Questions. Politicians as comedians and comedians as politicians.

Nowadays the two have merged into one. Boris Johnson. Donald Trump. Liz Truss. We've entered a world where You Couldn't Make It Up. In Trump's Cabinet we have a Health Secretary who is a vaccine sceptic, once sawed the head off a whale and keeps a fridge full of roadkill. An Education Secretary whose qualifications include heading up a big Worldwide Wrestling franchise and wanting to get rid of the Department of Education. (Though her biggest qualification may be the $21m she reportedly donated to Trump's campaign). And a President who at least has managed to hold on to his convictions. All 34 of them. The most convicted President in History. Totally.

For Tim and Mary, this is grist to the mill. Each day brings new comic possibilities. In this book, they tell of their journey into writing and a decade or more of taking topical events and turning them into comedy- for their own sanity, as much as anybody else's. To paraphrase the infamous "Scottish Play" by the immortal William Shakespeare, subject of Boris Johnson's yet-to-materialise book and close personal friend of Donald J Trump, it's "a tale told by two idiots, full of sound and Rory, and signifying nothing…"

…other than a delight in finding fun in a mad and desperate world.

Rory Bremner

February 2025

Introduction

An Englishman, a Welshman and a Scotsman walk into a library and realise they're in the wrong joke. Embarrassed, they leave, go to the trendy wine bar down the road and get into a fight with the European Union. The Englishman leaves in a huff taking the Welshman and the Scotsman with him.

Time passes, and the door opens again.

A genius walks into the bar. He sees two idiots sitting at a table and hears them laughing. He orders a drink and wonders what's so funny. Are they laughing at him? To be fair, that's what he often invites people to do.

No, they're just giddy on how ridiculous life is. The genius agrees and has made it his business to shine a light on all the nonsense. The genius and the two idiots collaborate and somehow, their words bring a little poetic order into the world.

In 'Two Idiots and a Genius' we tell lots of jokes while examining the role that political satire plays in what some have called our 'post-truth' society. We do this by reproducing some of the material we've written from 2012 to present, with reference to the news stories that were current at the time. We also added plenty of new jokes as we thought of them because, quite frankly, we can't help ourselves.

Rory writes most of his own material but like all performers, he takes inspiration from others. We're fortunate to be part of the small team that chips in on a regular basis. It's a joyful process, even when it's hard work. This material doesn't just appear out of thin air, like most creatives there are times when the jokes flow and times when we shut ourselves in a dark room and dig deep, fuelled by Jaffa Cakes (Mary) and chocolate buttons (Tim). We love it. Rory is incredibly rewarding to write for. He's a humble genius, fiercely intelligent and a warm-hearted gentleman.

Most of you will know Rory as an impressionist, although he's actually a genius of many talents. His ability to mimic the voices of a multitude of political leaders is legendary. He adopts their characteristics and seems to become them. He's a pretty damned good standup when he's just being himself, too. A graduate of King's College, London, where he studied for a BA in Modern Languages, he also translates German and French opera for fun and for professional opera companies. Add in numerous acting roles in many stage productions and you've got a national treasure that we're fortunate to call 'Boss' and friend.

Now, we're not performers, we're writers, putting Tim's Politics Degree and Mary's Creative Writing MA to good use, so we don't even try to play with the voices. But you can! Give it go, just for fun. See how Trumpian you can become, baffle as Boris, giggle as you go. We dare you. Send your best impersonations to Tim & Mary Fowler @ pleasedon't.com. Even better, if you're at one of Rory's fantastic gigs and we happen to be there, come over and say 'hello'. We'd love to meet you!

In conclusion, if you're a fan of Rory Bremner, love a bit of comedy and political satire or are interested in the process of writing comedy for stage, television and radio, this is the book for you.

Chapter One

We're all in it together?

2012

(The News Quiz – BBC Radio 4, April-May 2012)

"Right wing Tory MP Nadine Dorries explains that when she called Cameron and Osborne 'a couple of arrogant posh boys', she meant it as a compliment."

We begin our tale in the spring of 2012. It's a fair while ago now and a great deal of murky political water has flowed under many burning bridges, so let's remind you of how things stood back then.

We're two years into the Tory/Lib Dem coalition government, brought to power in 2010, in an election that put an end to the New Labour project and left many in North London crying into their wheatgrass smoothies. The coalition is an uneasy marriage, unravelling like a cheap knitted blue and yellow blanket, between those "arrogant posh boys" David Cameron and George Osborne and the 'knit-your-own-policies' Liberal Democrats, led by Nick Clegg. Everyone had loved Clegg for twenty-four hours after the first debate of the 2010 election campaign where he'd charmed the electorate and hadn't yet morphed into Cameron's starved of affection puppy. Put your hand up if you remember "#IAgreeWithNick"? No, us neither.

The effects of the 2008 Financial Crisis, and the global recession it caused, continue to have a profound impact on both the economy and daily life. There's still an awful lot of pretty much justified anger at a banking industry seemingly without morals, hubris or shame which caused the crisis through a toxic cocktail* of greed and stupidity. It won't surprise you to learn that much of what we write about in this book is caused by one or both of those perennial bugbears of human existence.

*Toxic Cocktail recipe: take 2 measures of Old Vlad's Potato Vodka, one dash bitters, add a handful of sour grapes. Shake over crushed dreams and garnish with Ed Balls of melon. Drink alone in a dark room, thinking dark thoughts until the numbness sets in. Currently available at the House of Commons Bar for the princely sum of one GP appointment, a Waitrose delivery slot and your granny's false teeth.

Figure 1: available in all overpriced bars.

However, fear not! It's not all doom and gloom as British manufactured car sales are up by the end of the year. Bafflingly, most are Ford Fiestas, allegedly sold with a pair of lucky furry dice hanging from the rear-view mirror. Not driven by bankers, we believe.

In the 1800s, Charles Dickens – one of our favourite social satirists - spooked Scrooge into mending his greedy, wealth hoarding ways but sadly, that was only work of fiction, like most election manifestos. There's little evidence that trickle-down economics have ever really worked to fill empty bellies and warm cold bodies. A bit like leaking incontinence pads worn by misers, us paupers end up covered in the wealthy folk's mess. It's untenable (silly pun, sorry).

While we're talking about rich peoples' excrement, let's return to Spring 2012. David Cameron is embroiled in a noisy row about the exorbitant bonuses paid out to Stephen Hester, CEO of the then publicly owned Royal Bank of Scotland. In 2008, as Leader of the Opposition, Cameron had vocally campaigned for former RBS CEO, Sir Fred Goodwin (known popularly as "Fred the Shred", due to his rather gung-ho attitude to record-keeping and his fondness for disposing of inconvenient pieces of paper), to be 'stripped of his Honours' after RBS had been bailed out to the tune of £45.5 billion due to having a small issue with risk management. The government took a majority stake in the ailing bank, bought three million scratchcards, and put a tenner on West Ham to win the FA Cup while they were at it.

Four years on, the Coalition are forcing austerity on the masses and Cameron is now noticeably no longer speaking out about 'the need for moral markets' which had drawn too much attention to Tory immoral markets touting cash for honours, amongst other dodgy deals.

David Cameron and George Osborne are fond of saying 'we're all in this together' but this is very much at odds with huge bankers' bonuses, their own personal wealth and the economic reality being experienced by the bulk of the population.

Q: What do you call an old Etonian without a plum job? A: Dead.

Lack of trust in government, and in politicians as a species, is a theme we'll revisit often in these pages, and it's worth remembering that Cameron and Osborne would be two of the leading figures trying to convince the electorate to remain in the EU in 2016. Of which, you won't be surprised to hear, much, much more later.

This is an opportunity to talk about *how* we write satire.

It's a very good question that we're often asked but our answer is perhaps an unsatisfying if accurate one: *it depends*. With shows like the *News Quiz* or *Breaking the News*, a set of briefing notes lands in our inbox 48-72 hours before recording and writing becomes a question of riffing off those notes, looking for wordplay or broken logic that can be the basis of a joke.

For example, for the Cameron/Osborne story we produced these:

"We're all in this together" is almost self-satirising: the fact that Cameron and Osborne feel they have to say this presupposes that it isn't true. If we really were all in it together it would not need to be said.

Providing 'this' is an Olympic-sized swimming pool full of manure, then yes, we're in the same place as you, Mr Cameron.

They think it's the Dunkirk spirit, but they come across more like posh kids on a gap year, drumming up support to get someone else to dig a well.

From this government it sounds more like a flu pandemic warning than a reassurance

(2024 note: well, well, well!)

We're all in this together, shouts Dave, as he lowers himself into the first lifeboat, and then transfers on to his yacht.

I'm not quite sure what the 'this' we're all supposed to be together in is? A barely controlled state of panic? Denial? Despair?

Oddly enough, "a barely controlled state of panic" is not a bad description of how having to be funny in the face of a looming deadline can feel. Of course, the more often you do it, the better you get* and the repeated structures of shows like The News Quiz or Breaking the News (BBC Radio Scotland) become a kind of comfort blanket: you know how to do this. Pick the laptop up, stop procrastinating on social media and get typing.

(*health and safety note: this is not true of falling off your bicycle)

The other stories for that episode of the News Quiz revolve around the Cash for Access row, an early entry in the litany of what will become referred to as "Tory sleaze". Peter Cruddas MP has lost his job after being videoed by undercover journalists offering to arrange meetings with the Prime Minister and others for the small consideration of £250,000. Thus:

How much do I have to pay to avoid meeting Cameron?

Free Clegg with every Cameron. Actually, just free Clegg. The "Lib Dem One". Which may also be the number of voters they have left.

Government to introduce minimum unit pricing for political bribes. Exchange rate to be one backhander = five backbenchers.

Let he who is without sin cast the first Bernie Ecclestone

New Tory motto "Looking gift horses in the mouth".

For £5k you can have dinner with Eric Pickles – for £10k he'll let you eat some of it.

Is Nick Clegg on list of people who paid to have dinner with Dave?

There are a couple of interesting points here: firstly, one of the particular joys of writing for Rory is that we have the endless toybox of his impressions to play with – for example, as above, any opportunity to use his wonderful David Cameron impression is too good to miss.

The other point is that we often look to combine stories: around this time there is consideration of the introduction of minimum unit prices for alcohol. Combining this with the Cash for Access story gives us the idea of minimum pricing for bribes, and bang! Satire.

…and boy there is a lot to satirise in the spring of 2012: the government is introducing a benefit cap to limit the total amount of benefits that unemployed families could receive:

Government explain that the media have misunderstood the 'benefit cap'. It's actually a real cap (preferably cloth) that people on benefits will have to wear and doff at their betters:

Figure 2: The Tories might prefer a compulsory contraceptive to stop the poor buggers from breeding so damn much. Not doing a picture of that one.

We're back to the posh boys wagging their gold-plated fingers at the poor: it's a satirical open goal, and we don't pass those up.

In similar vein, Education Secretary Michael Gove is keen to reform Sex Education in schools, having got hold of the idea that higher performing students 'had less sex'. Grammatically correct but otherwise barmy. Now, we're not ones to start conspiracy theories, but it's interesting to note that despite looking like a nightmarish version of Pinocchio, debate remains open as to whether, or not, Gove is a real boy.

Gove thinks that better qualified teenagers don't have sex. Precisely how dull a time did he have at Oxford?

A levels are getting easier, though if Michael Gove has his way, the pupils won't be.

So, that's Romeo and Juliet off the curriculum, then.

Gove announces boost for plumbing industry as cold showers are to be installed in all secondary schools.

Bike sheds to be relocated against walls to prevent any posterior shenanigans.

Along comes another gift of an idea being floated as a policy by the Department for Environment, Food and Rural Affairs which seems ripe for satire: compulsory microchipping of dogs. This does eventually become enshrined in UK law in 2016, four years after we've had our fun with it. Thanks for giving us time to write some jokes, DEFRA.

Will this go hand in hand with the setting up of a Rex Offenders Register?

Cameron *on having Francis Maude* microchipped: 'he has this awful habit of just running up to journalists and saying the first thing that comes into his head. Of course I have no such problems with my bitch, Clegg'*

Apple fans will be able to have their dog dyed in one a of a range of colours, pay four times as much for the chip and buy another almost identical dog 10 months later.

These three lines are good examples of types we often find useful: the silly pun ("Rex Offenders"), the what-do-they-really-think political satire ("Francis Maude") and the socio-cultural satire ("Apple dogs"). The essential point is that satire **must be funny**.

Make people laugh and you've earned the right to make them think. That's the plan, anyway – and fortunately governments and politicians of all shades and types provide plenty of material to both laugh at and think about.

*For those of us who have erased the easily forgotten Francis Maude from our memories, he was a Tory Minister who was prone to making verbal gaffes and then walking away from the noxious stink they caused, blaming the unchipped dog. Notably, during the 2012 fuel crisis, he advised drivers to store jerry cans full of petrol in their garages. The General Secretary of the Fire Brigades' Union took time out from working as a stripogram (joke), sighed loudly and said it was "dangerous and illegal advice". We assume Maude then rushed to hide the fireworks, matches and dry sticks he had stored next to his petrol stash.

The period of time this book covers is notable in a number of ways: we had a Tory government almost entirely throughout - something few would have predicted in 2012 - and the decade contained an unprecedented number of referenda: bear in mind we'd already had the Proportional Representation Referendum in 2011, which had been the Lib Dem's price for propping up Cameron's government and had ended in defeat for the reformers, not least due to confusing questions like this one:

"Would you be in favour of voting slips being made from recycled elderly people? Oh, and a fairer election system for the Lib Dems - but you hate them, right, so vote no, yeah?"

Or something like that. It might as well have been.

The Brexit Referendum is still four years away, lurking like a hungry great white shark off a crowded beach, but first we have "Indyref", the Scottish independence referendum on the horizon. The SNP, led by Alex Salmond, have campaigned hard on the issue of holding a referendum. On the back of this, they secure a thirty-two seat majority in the 2011 Scottish parliamentary elections and have a big shiny mandate that they are understandably keen to use.

BBC Reporter: *Home Secretary Theresa May warns that an independent Scotland could face the prospect of checks at the border. Is that a promise? Scots say they'll accept cash as well but only in Scottish notes. No change will be given.*

Inevitably we've written hundreds of lines like these, responses to individual events, people or policies. What we want to do in this book is use them to tell the story of the last twelve tumultuous years and perhaps find how satire needs to respond to an increasingly disturbed and disturbing world. We'll even write some brand new jokes for you, because we're all heart and also because the book would have been too short without them. Ahem. Satire has to reflect the culture and society in which it operates, so we'll talk about that, too. It can be a very powerful tool, as Aristophanes, Jonathan Swift, Charles Dickens, Anthony Trollope and Dorothy Parker, amongst others, have ably demonstrated. We're small fry in that company but we're pretty confident that we'll make you laugh – and yes, we hope you'll allow us to make you think, too.

Chapter Two

Olympic'n'mix.

2012

(More for the News Quiz: BBC Radio 4, June-July & September-October 2012)

*"Every time I see Sunderland racing to be first to declare at elections I think: there's a city that **really** misses 'It's A Knockout'". (Google it if you're too young to have wasted many hours watching Boomers scramble over giant inflatables in a race to win a pair of furry dice for their Ford Fiestas.)*

2012 is a very busy year, not least because the UK is hosting the Olympics for the first time since 1948. Preparations have been dogged by construction delays and budget overspends and there is more than the usual amount of very British cynicism in the air. When the *News Quiz* is broadcast in late April there is a story about the forced eviction of houseboat residents near to the Olympic Park in East London – action described by the Guardian (and others) as "Social Cleansing". Oh, we were *so* grateful they called it that:

NEW! Social cleanser from Cillit Bang! BANG, and the poor are gone!

Cameron: *"gosh, yes, we have a social cleanser. On some kind of scheme, comes in twice a week, simply MARVELLOUS with the children"*
Boris Johnson *(Mayor of London at this time) "The Olympic Spirit is*

one of taking part. Which is why we're taking part of London's population and moving it to Stoke-on-Trent."

Moving on to bloodsports, not *currently* an Olympic event (although "mass shooting" seems a shoe-in next time the Games are in the USA), the Leveson Inquiry into press ethics and intrusion is being particularly entertaining with an array of witnesses being called including Piers Morgan, Rebekah Brooks (former *News of the World* editor and "neighbour" of David Cameron – *neighbour* in the Cotswolds sense of being two miles away in the next mansion), Tony Blair and Alaistair Campbell. It perhaps reaches its zenith when Rupert Murdoch testifies and says…

…that he doesn't "know many politicians", which is confirmed enthusiastically by the hundreds of politicians around the world who know him.

Despite poll numbers that must be giving him nightmares, Nick Clegg continues to revel in the title of Deputy Prime Minister. In 2012, having previously failed to get proportional representation adopted, he picks the next thing he's going to fail to do: reforming the House of Lords:

There will be special dispensation and automatic peerages for unelectable unpopular ex-deputy Prime Ministers.

Deputy PM Cluggle denied all reports that Lord Voldemort would be taking up his seat in the new chamber. 'He has not returned'

The irony is that with the makeup of the current government, the so-called House of Commons is actually considerably posher than the Lords.

This – or anything else the government tries to do – doesn't really capture the public imagination (understatement) and in May, in a desperate attempt to rekindle voter enthusiasm, the coalition decide to carry out a relaunch. Though I'm not sure you can rekindle something that wasn't on fire in the first place. Indeed, the whole country is positively waterlogged following the wettest April on record and even the Easter Bunny has gone into hiding, last seen covered in chocolate, surrounded by brightly coloured foil wrappers. (Note from Tim: that was you, Mary.) (Note from Mary: guilty as charged.)

The coalition choose to hold the relaunch in – wait for it - a tractor factory which cheers our Tim up no end and awakens his previously unknown inner Stalinist:

<stirring Soviet-era military music plays>

TRIUMPH IN GRANTHAM!

Great news, comrades! At the Thatchograd (formerly Grantham) Tractor Factory, comrades Camerov and Cleggovic triumphantly revealed their Glorious Five-Minute Plan and declared eternal brotherhood between them, or until next week at least.

Following on the triumphant re-election of Comrade Boris as First Secretary of Londograd this is truly a splendid week for the PoshitBuro....

Figure 3: David Cameron finally standing up to bankers.

In fact, things are going so badly for the Tory/Lib Dem Coalition it seems *inconceivable* that Labour won't triumph convincingly at the next election, whenever it is. I mean, of course they will, right? We feel moved by this to simultaneously plagiarise and ruin one of the finest works of Alfred, Lord Tennyson:

How Much To Charge For The Shite Brigade

Half a term, half a term,
Half a term squandered,
All in the valley of debt
Rode the three hundred.

Theirs not to reason why,
Theirs not to hinder Sky,

Theirs but to sell and buy:
Into the valley of Government
Rode the three hundred.

UKIP to the right of them,
Labour to left of them,
Leveson in front of them
Hack'd and advis'd
Kotowed to Murdochs all
Watched the poll numbers fall.
Into the jaws of Miliband, Ed,
Harman, Cooper, Skinner and Balls
Rode the three hundred...

This is a device we'll return to again and again (or it's a dead horse that we happily continue to flog, depending on your point of view) - rewriting something well known to fit a particular story. Tom Lehrer is one of our comedy heroes and no-one did this better than him. If you're not familiar with Lehrer's brilliantly satirical songs, run to YouTube or your music streaming service of choice and listen to some of them. We beg of you. *"Poisoning Pigeons in the Park"* is a good place to start.

Our 'Charge of the Light Brigade' parody is also notable as being the first of far, far(age) too many mentions of UKIP, a political party that, by one name or another, sticks in our satirical throats like days' old phlegm. Damn them. Cough, cough. Pass the spittoon.

Amongst the many things that provide particularly good opportunities for satirical comedy are when things are going badly wrong. Whether it be mismanaged elections, white elephant infrastructure projects and – perhaps best of all - financial crises, because they do seem to at least begin with bad people having deservedly bad things happen to them.

The wet spring of 2012 is kind in this respect, offering a "double dip" recession in the UK and a Presidential election in France between notoriously short incumbent Nicolas Sarkozy and challenger Francoise Hollande, who nobody refers to as Frankie Dutch, which is disappointing. The right in France is becoming politically significant again in the shape of Marine le Pen – who is far-right royalty as the daughter of firebrand Jen Marie le Pen - and mainstream politicians ignore it at their peril.

The recession is being laid firmly at the door of the Coalition, especially the posh 'pin up' boy band of Cameron and Osborne, to be seen gravely posing at every opportunity. Thankfully, they don't release a charity* single and appear on Top of the Pops, or as the centre spread in Smash Hits.

*(*Charity? The Tories?? Pull the other one.)*

It's unfair to call it a double dip recession, I'm sure Nick Clegg was involved somehow too.

Not surprised the economy's shrunk. Most things shrink when they get soaking wet.

Depressing thing is, we can't even do a nice little double dip joke like we could with Greece and hummus and taramasalata. What would we have? Tomato Ketchup and Salad Cream? Doesn't quite have the same ring. Or taste.

Sarkozy courts the right wing vote by taking a step to the right. And another one. And another one, thus moving him a very short way.

Rumours that Sarkozy is attempting to "court the right wing" produces French media frenzy outside Nadine Dorries' house.

If Hollande wins in France, Dawn French to stand for Dutch Parliament.

Hollande won, by the way, but as we write Dawn has yet to show any political ambitions. Shame as she'd do it the M&S way and we'd all be gifted posh undies and she'd put on a nice spread of (political) party food.

Of course, there's more to life than politics and thankfully the media reflect this, giving us so many more things to write jokes about. Around this time there has been a spate of thefts from supermarkets' newish self-service tills. A survey suggests that up to a third of those questioned confess to having done this. It's worth bearing in mind that that's roughly the same proportion of the electorate that would go on to vote Leave in 2016. Just saying.

Tesco and Sainsburys issue statements saying that they now regret following Plain English Campaign recommendation to refer to their self-service tills as "Help Yourself Points".

Self-service till theft is like looting for middle class people. Slipping a tin of anchovies or a few extra kumquats into the bag next to the bottle of Dom Perignon and the tin of Pedigree Chum for your labradoodle Percy.

If a third admit to doing it, that pretty much means the other 2/3 are doing it and don't want to admit it.

"Unexpected item in bagging area" is phrase you don't want to hear in a supermarket, airport or particularly a hospital.

What the media report, and how they research and report it, is very much in the news thanks to the ongoing Leveson Inquiry into press ethics. Blimey, that's a deep old rabbit hole and no mistake. The phone hacking scandal in 2011 had already brought down the *News of the World* (albeit reinvented as the *strikingly* similar *Sun on Sunday*) and the Motorman inquiry of 2003 had revealed that the Metropolitan Police repeatedly used private investigators to pass confidential information to national newspapers, which was shocking but not remotely surprising to anyone who'd been paying even a little bit of attention. Rory was starting a new series of his "Tonight with…." Show on BBC Radio 4 and asked Tim to have a think about why any of it mattered:

The distorted relationship between politicians and the press and between press and police has been like the troubled and troubling relative we don't talk about but who hovers in the background of the family photos: a ghostly pre-dementia Claudius, demanding loudly that we notice and respond.

Think of any recent high profile murder case. The media timeline will go something like this: a suspect is arrested. Within hours, detailed personal information about them is in the newspapers and on their websites. The source, at least in part, is clearly the police as no-one else could have access to that depth of information so quickly. This alone would be troubling in judicial terms but, when there are also payments being made to police by the press, it takes on a very much more worrying aspect.

We keep thinking of that red top headline "It was the Sun wot won it" referring to the Conservative election win in 1992. The newspaper had famously ridiculed Neil Kinnock's Labour Party throughout the election campaign and had devoted its front page on election day to a giant headline which read:

"If Kinnock wins today, will the last person to leave Britain please turn out the lights"

Thereby condemning Kinnock to only one mention in this book.

Viewed through Leveson's binoculars this kind of journalism takes on a different and more sinister slant. Perhaps "It was the Sun what done it" might be a more accurate headline.

Do we really believe this stops at News International titles? Very noticeably, The Mirror is keeping its head down for fear the scandal may reflect badly on them.

"Mirror, Mirror, behind the paywall, who's the biggest hacker of you all?"

The Motorman investigation details countless breaches of privacy laws across all forms of communication – Leveson has barely touched on email hacking - to the extent that even the inquiry and the Culture, Media and Sport parliamentary committee report may only address the tip of the iceberg. It remains unclear just who (other than Piers Morgan, naturally) is on the SS Titanic Porkies, steaming its way towards the looming iceberg of hubris and well-deserved disaster.

Sub-question: Who does it matter TO?

There's a real issue here of this being a much bigger story within the Westminster Bubble and associated hangers-on (i.e. Twitter/ Bloggers/ Political comedy writers) than it is "out there", in the real world. Is there any evidence that it's affected the local election results? Can it really bring

Cameron's government down? If it did, would the country at large scratch the dandruff from its collective head and wonder what the hell was going on?

This is not to belittle the seriousness of the situation but it's worth pointing out that Leveson almost never (to date) features in the upper half of the most-read stories on mainstream news sites.

*Belief in the political process is already at such a low level that Leveson will not perhaps cause more than a ripple. It's simply **not** what matters most to people. The NHS, tax, wages, jobs, housing, food prices, security **are**.*

This leads quite nicely to a related question: does satire matter? If it does, why? You can imagine what our answer to the first question is, but here it is anyway: in a free society, it is terribly important that the powerful are brought to account. Yes, the ballot box is the primary way of doing that but that's only once every four or five years and election campaigns aren't known for their nuance. In fact, in this respect they've become much, much worse over the last decade. More on that later. Plus, for a multitude of reasons, electoral turnout in the UK is on the decline and there must be a better way of engaging our population in political discourse.

We believe that satire can plug that gap and the more outrageous the behaviour of the powerful, the more important it becomes: Donald Trump's (first) term as president produced a flowering of satire in the US on both new media and old, mainstream and niche alike. Of course, the old adage that there's no such thing as bad publicity has to be borne in mind, and the image of old orange face plastered all over our television screens is a form of cortical indoctrination that will need gallons of mind-bleach to erase.

However, we firmly believe that burying our heads in oil rich sand will only lead to political deafness and gritty nostrils. So, we write, write and write and hope that you'll read. Please?

Figure 4: Auguste Rodin's immortal sculpture "what's the bloody point of satire?".

As George Orwell said, "in a time of deceit, telling the truth is a revolutionary act.", and Orwell knew a thing or two about those.

And if satire can make us, and you, laugh at the same time as opening all of our minds to something beyond the accepted wisdom, or folly, all the better.

Chapter Three

American elections and other alternative realities
2012.

(Tonight with Rory Bremner, BBC Radio 4, Summer 2012 & Rory on Tour, September-December 2012)

*"The Boss is on Tour. No, not Bruce Springsteen. Although Rory's a whizz at karaoke."**

*Allegedly.

When Rory's on tour, the writing routine changes. There's normally a new venue every other day or so and in 2012 that means researching and writing a few lines about the town or city where the gig is plus writing as much material as possible about whatever's in the news. Typically, the first half of the show is rewritten on the fly as the tour progresses. Any kind of creativity is like a muscle: you need to exercise it to keep it working, and in that sense the tours are great. Overcoming the fear of the blank page every couple of days is very satisfying and keeps us from seizing up. Here's an example from May 2012 when Rory is in Newark:

Newark has both the UK's largest cream cake factory and a sugar beet refinery. I'm glad I got the chance to come here before Jamie Oliver has it closed down.

(At this time, Jamie Oliver is campaigning to make school dinners healthier, with some parents feeding chips to their grease-deprived offspring through school fences?)

In the civil war, Newark was besieged by parliamentary forces. I think we all know how that feels now.

People told me that Newark is an anagram of an insulting name, but I tried for ages and couldn't make 'Nick Clegg' out of the letters.

Also in the news, David Cameron is at the G8 summit at Camp David in Maryland (where he's eating chocolate chip cookies, presumably) the US Election campaign is underway and the Eurozone debt problems continue, with the Greek economy on the verge of collapse. Or is it Portugal? Ireland? It's hard to keep track. Another week, another Eurozone crisis.

Cameron: *I thought that G8 was text speak for what you open to get into a field...*

G8 meetings are like Star Wars prequels, the more of them there are, the less impressive they get, and the harder it becomes to remember why you liked them in the first place*

What can the G8 actually do? They can agree not to disagree or agree to agree, or agree to agreeing to disagree, or disagree about whether they agree or not.

The end-of-summit communique is terse: "We affirm our interest in Greece remaining in the Eurozone" which is about as informative as "We affirm our interest in continuing to breathe". It went on to state the G8's commitment to motherhood and apple-based desserts.

What would a President Romney be like? Would Cameron take him to see The Marsh when he visits?

First there were holes in the Ozone layer, now the Eurozone's full of them. It's just like an episode of The Twilight Z....oh, never mind.

The Greek government is acting like a bailout would be a feta worse than death. Not so much quantitative easing as quantitative cheesing.

Looking back with the benefit of 2024 hindsight, the G8 has been the G7 for some time since Russia was disinvited, the UK isn't part of the Eurozone in any sense whatsoever, Obama won easily against Romney and extraordinarily, *Lord* David Cameron is still mixing in the highest diplomatic circles as Foreign Secretary:

Figure 5: : Contrary to Professor Cox's statements, things have actually been getting steadily worse.

(We're assuming here that when the Large Hadron Collider was switched on in 2010 it projected us into an alternate universe where all this weird shit became normal. Somewhere out there in the Multiverse, Hilary's in her second term, David Miliband is celebrating a decade in power and we're still in the EU. Hopefully, the Tories are trailing somewhere behind the Mothers' Union as a political force. The more you think about this idea the more sense it makes. And we can blame Brian Cox.)

Ten things that may have actually happened since 2012 which are weirder than David Cameron being Foreign Secretary:

1. The London Olympics were a huge success and nothing much went wrong. I mean, really?
2. Trump 2016
3. Brexit
4. Trump 2020
5. Boris is Prime Minister. FFS.
6. Entire world grinds to halt due to a) Covid and b) stupidity. 'Leader' of free world suggests drinking bleach and signs a exclusive brand deal with Domestos.
7. Did Paddington kill the queen with poisoned marmalade sandwiches? Much, much less likely scenarios fill the internet, mostly involving the royal artist formerly known as Prince Harry. We did say this is a list of things that may have happened…
8. Liz Truss is Prime Minister for 50 days but still manages to be the first PM since Churchill to bridge the reign of two monarchs.
9. England are good at cricket, thanks to two New Zealanders.
10. Trump 2024

You see? Craaaaaazy stuff. Alternate Universe. Boris is a Higgs Boson. Or a Higgs Bozo. You heard it here first.

Speaking of crazy, at the time of writing (April 2024) George Galloway has just won a by-election in Rochdale, showing that hysteria/history does indeed repeat itself. In 2012 we were writing jokes about him winning Bradford West for the 'Respect the Stop the War I Hate Tony Blair Coalition Rebellion sponsored by Dreamies cat treats' or something of that ilk.

George Galloway scraps Respect Coalition because there isn't anyone he respects and no-one wants to be in a coalition with him. Bad kitty.

Ian Duncan Smith, the least popular man with three names since Attila the Hun or Vlad the Impaler, is Welfare Secretary and announces the closure of five Remploy factories, which create job opportunities uniquely for disabled workers who might not otherwise find employment, undeserving swine that he probably thinks they are.

In an attempt to improve his image after Remploy gaffe, Ian Duncan Smith embarks on forty-date beggar-kicking tour of the UK, says he hates his mother and bans manufacture of apple pies.

After suggesting that the disabled should 'get proper jobs', numerous disabled charities suggest that IDS should sod off and do the same.

…and this is ten years after Theresa May warned the party conference that some people – shock horror - saw the Tories as the "nasty party". IDS obviously felt that only "some people" thinking that simply wasn't good enough. If you think that's ridiculous, a 2023 article in the *Spectator* (former editor B Johnson esq.) was headlined:

"Could a return to its 'nasty party' roots save the Tories?"

Sometimes satire writes itself. Not often, but we take what we can get.

And so, 2012 rolls on to what is for many the highlight of the year: the London Olympics. Despite an inauspicious start (flying the flag of North Korea at a football match in Glasgow featuring South Korea - whoopsie) it is, to even the most jaded eyes (i.e. Tim) a resounding success. The newly christened *Team GB* rake in the medals in a huge range of sports and make bona fide stars of its 29 Gold Medallists. Gold post-boxes spring up across the land, and everyone emails their friends to tell them about it. Security at the Olympics is understandably tight, with missile batteries installed on high buildings around the Olympic Park. If that now seems a little paranoid or over the top, it's worth remembering that the UK had been awarded the games the day before the 7/7 bomb attacks in London. As LP Hartley wrote:

"The past is a foreign country. They can't make tea there."

Hang on, that's not right…

Rory was on the News Quiz again just before the games started and was asked to consider how the flame might be lit:

Blair: *I would do it, but Gordon would throw a bucket of water over it rather than let me. Miserable spoilsport.*

Prince Charles: *I'll get the wife to do it with her lighter.*

Eastenders have offered to film Dot Cotton flicking a fag butt into the torch.

Maybe they'll light it with one of the anti-aircraft missiles.

Not surprised by the Korean flag thing. Glaswegians think everywhere else is 'South'

End of chapter. You can now have the cup of tea we just made you want and try to remember who the hell those twenty-nine gold medallists were.

Chapter Four

Saving Mr Banker.

2012

(The News Quiz & Rory on Tour, November 2012)

David Cameron: *"As Prime Minister, I welcome and rejoice in the spirit of the Olympics and Paralympics and the success of Team GB and will not belittle that by taking political advantage of it, whatever tough times lie ahead for Coalition GB."*

Nick Clegg: *"Being in Government is a marathon, not a sprint and I'm confident of clearing all the hurdles that lie ahead. I'll get David to pick up the ones we've knocked over so far. Medals, please."*

Form an orderly queue to tell Nick that there aren't any hurdles in a marathon.

With the feel-good days of the Olympic summer behind us, we finish off the last Magnum from the freezer as the media return to their more normal autumnal obsessions: Party Conferences and attendant scandals, and the annual game of "who's going to be on I'm a Celebrity, Get Me Out of Here"? Tory MP Nadine Dorries obliges by covering both bases, with Tory Chief Whip Andrew Mitchell providing the political scandal. He has an altercation with police on duty at the gates to Downing Street after they fail to recognise him. Not much hurts the parliamentary ego more than that and Mitchell allegedly swears at Mr Plod, calls the assembled group "plebs" and is also alleged to have said a considerably less polite version of "Don't you know who I am, my good fellow?". The leaking of police logs (subsequently revealed to have been altered, naughty Mr Plod) to the press deepens the crisis and shows that the ongoing Leveson inquiry has no shortage of new material. Mitchell resigns from the cabinet later in the month and disappears into further obscurity, an act which adds another huge greasy chip to his shoulder and to his bruised ego.

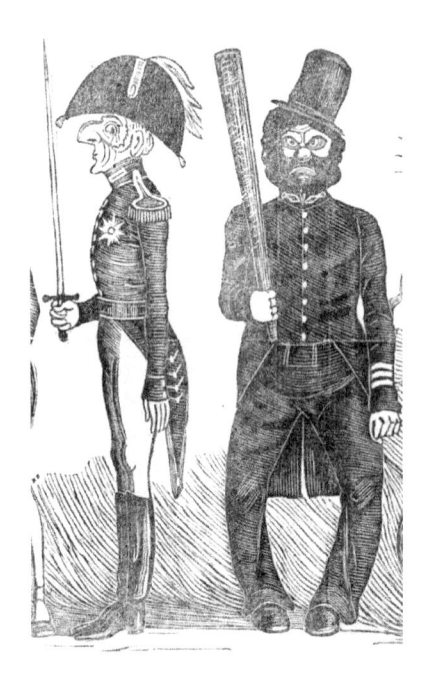

Figure 6: How Andrew Mitchell (left) viewed the "Battle of Downing Street"

Ironically, if Andrew Mitchell had asked me who the feck he was I wouldn't have known either.

Vince Cable described himself at the Lib Dem conference as "just a pleb." Of course, in his case it's an acronym: Politician Leaving, Early Bedtime.

When Nadine Dorries was asked to go on a live TV show involving sadistic challenges and gloating hosts, she thought they meant Newsnight.

Nadine Dorries misheard the title - she thought it was 'I'm for celibacy, get me out of here'.

There's a good deal of schadenfreude in the political classes at the spectacle of the BBC's two top news shows, Panorama and Newsnight (sorry, The One Show, you're not on the list) going hammer and tongs over who had known what, and when, about monstrous abuser Jimmy Saville.

It's been a month for great rivalries of our times.

Chelsea versus Manchester United

Corrie vs Eastenders

Obama vs Romney

Chips v diet

And, of course, the daddy of them all

Panorama Vs Newsnight.

Figure 7: Kirsty Wark and Fiona Bruce enjoy a frank exchange of views over the Panorama/Newsnight kerfuffle.

There's also been a cabinet reshuffle before the new parliamentary term which has gone to show that shuffling the pack doesn't always rule out a lousy deal. Newly minted Health secretary Jeremy Hunt casts himself in the role of Joker when he's revealed to be a believer in homeopathy:

We have in Jeremy Hunt a Health Minister who believes in homeopathy - I wonder if it'll lead him to water down the NHS reforms?

It could pave the way for News International to take over parts of the health service. They must think Hunt's arse shines out of the Sun.

In 2010, the Lib Dem's decision to go into Coalition with the Conservatives had not been a widely popular one, particularly when signature Lib Dem election promises on the environment and student loans were rapidly kicked into the parliamentary long grass, never to be seen again. Three by-elections in November 2012 give the electorate in Corby, Manchester Central and Cardiff South the chance to deliver a verdict, and it isn't good. Lib Dem support collapses in Manchester and they are behind UKIP in Corby. Ouch.

Following a disastrous showing in yesterday's elections, Lib Dems are in the bottom 2 and face a dance-off against UKIP in front of the judges. Strictly speaking (see what we did there), actually one judge. Lord Leveson.

Looks like hardly anyone agrees with Nick now.

With hindsight, it's possible to argue that Nick Clegg actually did the thing we say we want our politicians to do – put country before party. After the 2010 election, coalition talks with Gordon Brown's Labour had rapidly broken down. The UK economy – the world economy – was, to put it mildly, on fire in the toilet following the 2008 credit crunch and the global recession it caused. Another election – which would have followed quickly if no coalition had formed – would have created uncertainty and as we all know, that's anathema to those nervous little snowflakes in the City, who could see their massive salaries and even bigger bonuses melting away from grossly obscene to just mildly obscene.

Of course, maybe he was just another ambitious politician seduced by getting a posh job – in Nick's case, Deputy Prime Minister. He progressed to working for Meta/Facebook as "President of Global Affairs" so yeah, I think he might just have been swayed by a good job title. At present, there's no record of how many global affairs he's presided over.

2012 ends with the global economy firmly in recession (again) and much focus on the failure of Eurozone government gilts to generate affordable liquidity. Confused? Here's a handy explainer Tim wrote for "Tonight with Rory Bremner"

Banks don't do what you think they do.

Figure 8: An unusually deep banking metaphor by the standards of this book.

Joe Public: *They store my money in a big vault and lend it out to other people, don't they?*

No. Fundamentally, banks borrow from each other to buy investment products from other financial institutions, which they then sell to pension funds, private investors, and the same other banks they borrowed the money from in the first place.

JP: Why?

To **make money**, *of course. For every transaction that happens, a fee is charged, and there are hundreds of millions of transactions every day. Interest* rates have been so low that money borrowed short-term by the banks is basically free, and the banks know that the governments can't afford to let them fail so they have no reason not to behave like this. Retail banking (the stuff you do) is basically the bird picking fleas off the back of a charging elephant with diarrhoea.

JP: *what went wrong?*

The whole thing falls down when the investment products the banks borrow from each other to buy and sell turn out to be worth slightly less than diddly-squat. In 2008 it was subprime mortgages that no-one was ever going to pay back, packaged up into "safe" investments. Now it's government bonds from countries in the Eurozone: bonds, which for decades have been the ultimate safe investment because, like, the government will always be able to pay us back, right? Right?? Wrong, as it turns out. So now the international financial system is choked with bad government debt.

JP: *what's the solution?*

You're going to like this. Here's what the governments are doing. Strong economies (Germany, basically) are borrowing huge amounts of money from the markets via Government Bonds in order to shore up the failing Eurozone economies (because no-one wants to buy Greek debt because it'll never be paid back) and to give to the banks in those failing economies. And then the banks use the money to buy "safe" investments, like the very German government bonds that raised the money they're using to buy it. And then they package that debt up with bits of riskier debt they want off their books and sell it to your pension fund as "safe".

JP: Er....

Precisely.

Governments (mainly Germany again) are also injecting vast amounts of cash into the Eurozone economies to kickstart growth. Basically it's the Frankenstein theory. Shove a trillion volts through a corpse and when it twitches, Angela Merkel runs around the room shouting "it's alive! ALIVE!" What they're actually doing is creating another bubble, which like the south sea bubble, dot com bubble and housing bubble before, will do what bubbles always do.

JP: *Go on expanding steadily and safely forever and everything will be ok?*

No.

JP: *Oh.*

You see, and you're really going to like this: money isn't what you think it is.

JP: *It isn't?*

Money has no intrinsic value. Money is a promise. A £5 note used to be a promise that if you rocked up at your central bank and demanded it, they could give you £5 worth of gold. They wouldn't actually give it to you, of course, but in theory they could. This placed a limit on the amount of money that could exist in an economy based on the gold holdings in the central bank. Governments didn't like that because they wanted more money to use to do things that made people vote for them, build hospitals, cut tax, buy an independent nuclear deterrent.

JP: *A surefire vote winner.*

Yes. So, they took our economies off the gold standard and that allowed them to just invent money. Economy needs a kick up the backside? Want to pay for a big pre-election tax cut? Sell some government debt, which investors gobble up because it's safe, right?

JP: I can see where this is going.

I thought you might. Some governments even went so far as to sell off almost all their gold to raise even more money to spend.

JP: Who on earth would do such a ghastly, stupid, shortsighted thing?

Gordon Brown: That would be me. Sorry.

The upshot of this is that money has no intrinsic value. Its value is completely dependent on the health of the economy that issues it. Therefore, if an economy fails, the currency issued by that economy fails, which is why a single currency like the Euro with weak members (Greece again) is a really bad idea.

Gordon Brown: At least I got that one right.

So that's it, really. The value of the currency in your pocket is dependent on how willing the markets are to lend your government money at a non-crippling interest rate.

JP: Can I borrow a tenner?

You look southern European to me, so yes, but as long as you pay me back £20 tomorrow. I'll lend you the other £10 then so you can pay me back. Tell you what, I have a photo of a £10 note on my phone, how about I just airdrop you that? Sounds ridiculous, doesn't it? But this is effectively what's happening at the moment.

JP: I need a drink.

Here, have a tenner.

Tim's degree is in Politics but he was forced to study some economics too which made him terribly, terribly cross. You can tell, can't you?

Chapter Five

I got this long count calendar for Christmas and it's out of date already.

2013

(Rory on Tour, January-June 2013)

"I've a horrible suspicion it's taken longer to open the Stonehenge visitor centre than it took the aliens to build it in the first place."

"It's the end of the world as we know it, and I feel fine.." (REM)

We'll kick off 2013 by looking at something that definitively didn't happen in 2012: the end of the world.

The internet, that motherlode of bullshit and random nonsense even then, had been a-buzz (and a-twitter) with the Mayan Long Count calendar, which supposedly predicted that the world would end on the 21st of December 2012, apparently because it would run out of numbers. Or maybe, I don't know, perhaps people who lived 400 plus years ago had precisely zero fecking clue about predicting the future and failed to invent enough numbers - but that doesn't stop gullible idiots falling for the kind of hooey they fall for all the time (see InstaSnapFacegramTikX for literally billions of examples) (and the election of Das Fouluper-in-chief, Herr Trump. Ye gods.)

Mayans surprised we're still here. Land lucrative jobs writing weather reports for the Daily Express; predicting Amazon delivery times; and working for the credit ratings agencies.

So, in footballing terms, the Mayans have just done a typically theatrical and massive dive in the penalty area.

Mayan long count calendar actually predicted that a British man would win Wimbledon but end of world seemed more likely at the time.

Our view of the end of the world has changed: the four horsemen of the Apocalypse now are War, Famine, Death and No Wifi.

Andy Murray had won the gold medal in the Olympic singles tennis held at Wimbledon in 2012, and now in 2013, goes on to complete his full transition from Scottish to British by winning the Wimbledon Singles title itself. "Henman Hill" is rechristened "Murray Mount" while a campaign to change the name of Ben Nevis to "Andy's Alp" gets nowhere, unfortunately.

The Coalition's appetite for a minimalist tinkering kind of reform continues unabated, as does the influence of the Conservative Party's anti-EU activists. Michael Gove is very much on that wing of the Party and we have fun when, as Education Secretary, he decides to reform A Levels and we imagine the sort of questions they may feature.

Time of exam: 3 hours. Answer ALL questions. Or your benefits may be affected.

Complete the following sentences: community service, ASBO, 6 months Community Service, five years suspended.

"I would like to work for McDonalds". Discuss, with references.

If the answer is 6, is the question:

- *How many years did the Second World War last?*
- *How many wives did Henry VIII have?*
- *How many u-turns on the education reforms does Michael Gove make in a week, on average?*

Current affairs: discuss, without any valid or true examples whatsoever, the UK's membership of the EU. Write on one side of the argument only. Extra marks will be given for answers submitted on the side of a bus.

What year does Michael Gove think it is?

A) 1954

B) 1854

C) 1754

(you may tick all answers that apply)

A well-known international corporation turns over £3bn in the UK. How much corporation tax should they pay?

A) 25%

B) 1 %

C) a double decaff caramel macchiato. And a blueberry muffin.

Calculate, with reference to General Relativity, the curvature of space-time caused by corpulent Tory MP Eric Pickles.

Translate into English the updated National Curriculum.

Calculate, using imaginary numbers, the polling data for UKIP.

How much influence does Nick Clegg have on Government policy?

    A) Zilch
    B) Zero
    C) Who?

Media studies: with reference to the film 'Gentlemen Prefer Blondes', explain the appeal of Boris Johnson. Please. Really, what?

With reference to the Mayan Long Count Calendar, predict when governments will stop mucking around with exams. Please note, "when hell freezes over" is NOT an acceptable answer, even if it is true.

Write, using irrational numbers, how much you're prepared to pay me to pass this exam. Cash only. Euros not accepted..

Another thing the anti-EU wing of the Tory Party do is to promote a certain kind of rose-tinted Britishness: the flag, the Queen, picnics on the lawn and exploiting the riches of poor third world countries. In this sense, the media are The Right's useful idiots: the trope of calling TV shows the Great British something or other is reaching epidemic proportions: '…Menu';'…Bakeoff' and '…Sewing Bee' all gracing our ever-thinner televisions.

Rory asks Tim to reflect on this, and make some further suggestions:

Following the success of the Great British Bake Off, others are predictably intent on buying into this winning formula, with Heathrow rebranded as the Great British Take Off, Cumbria as the Great British Lake Off, The All-England suggestive chocolate eating competition as the Great British Flake Off and of course Who Wants to Be a Millionaire? as the Great British Fake Cough.

Almost everyone who calls themselves British has a different perception of it. It's used both by those who wish to unite and those who seek to divide – think of Danny Boyle's Olympic Guardianathon (he wrote and directed the left leaning opening ceremony) and the inevitable whingeing right wing responses to it. In fact, it seems appropriate that it ends in "-ish", such is the level of uncertainty associated with it.

To the English, British means "English", whilst to the Welsh, Scots and some of the Northern Irish "British" means…. "English" too.

Who gains from the concept of Britishness? Do the English have the most to gain given the concept of Englishness is, if anything, more fraught? Being British gives the English the best of the other component Nations, while still occasionally beating them at rugby. The English even lack their own proper mythology: King Arthur is Welsh and the Mail would want the real St George stopped at Calais as an illegal immigrant from North Africa. JRR Tolkien set out to create a mythology for England in his Middle Earth legendarium but even that turned out to be New Zealand after all.

Again, we see some early seeds of Brexit here: increasingly rabid Tory Eurosceptics and not so subtle appeals to a sense of mythic and very English Britishness. Still, the Tories are going to lose the next election so it doesn't matter, right?

Right?

In other news, ever felt like you've just had enough of your job and want to jack it in? Well, in 2013, the Pope agrees with you. On 28th February, Pope Benedict resigns, making him the first Pope ever not to die in office. Nice dodge, Ben.

Figure 9: Exclusive photo of the Pope's 2014 Hallowe'en costumer.

Perhaps the Pope's resigned to spend more time with his family, which would explain a lot.

Indeed.

This is discussed nowhere more than on Twitter, where 1000000000 Pope jokes are told within minutes of the announcement. Holy smoke, and all that. Another thing that gets Twitter riled up – rightly so – is Asda's decision to sell a "mental patient" costume as part of their Halloween range. Oh, Asda. Don't troll your customers.

Thanks, Asda, but I already have a mental patient costume. Today it's jeans and a fleece. Tomorrow I might wear a jumper.

The exponential growth of social media is changing every aspect of society although at the time no-one seems particularly bothered. What's the harm in people tweeting pictures of their breakfasts or how far they've run that day? What's the problem with Follow Friday, a lovely idea where lovely people share the accounts of other lovely people, so yet further lovely people can follow them?

Yes! It's Follow Friday! To be followed by Stalker Saturday and Restraining Order Sunday.

It's part of a trend of our lives becoming ever more technologically influenced. We had some concerns about this:

I see Google have bought a 'military robot company'. Can't remember if I saw it on the news or as a deleted scene on the Terminator 2 DVD.

I have a 4D printer. It takes a very long time to do anything and it all comes out warped.

Meanwhile across the Channel, our neighbours had real time problems:

French police have seized 1.3 tons of cocaine and will shortly hold a 32 hour long news briefing to discuss in forensic why everyone's out to get them.

Oui, monsieurs, c'est vrai.

Chapter Six

McReferendum.

2014

('Scotland, a Year Like No Other', December 2014, BBC1 Scotland.)

"So, the SNP had Salmond, and now they've got Sturgeon. Who's next? Captain Haddock?"

2014 is indeed a year like no other in Scotland: Glasgow hosts the Commonwealth Games, Gleneagles is the venue for the Ryder Cup, and most significantly there's the 143rd Annual Spot the Tory World Cup. Oh, hang on, that's not right: it's the Independence Referendum, isn't it? The SNP won a commanding majority in the Scottish Parliamentary elections in 2011 and have managed to get David Cameron to agree to holding a referendum on Scottish independence, which has been the SNP's raison d'etre* since they were founded.

(*Please note that we have received special written dispensation from the Foreign and Commonwealth Office of His Majesty's Government to use authentic French phrases while writing this book, under the terms of the Obsessively Petty Provisions of the UK Finally Leaving the EU Are You Happy Now Nigel Farage You Utter Bastard Act of 2019.)

Rory is a proud Scot and writes movingly of his final decision to vote no, despite the emotional pull of the idea of independence, particularly with a deeply unpopular government in Westminster:

"…if I am a Unionist, I'm a Scottish Unionist. My Union isn't the Union of Cameron, Osborne, Farage and Johnson. It's the Union of Gordon Brown, of Ming Campbell…of Robin Cook – and of Alex Salmond, of Scots working beyond Scotland to promote Scottish values." (Daily Telegraph, 11 September 2014)

This is also a list of some of Rory's, at this time, best impressions, which is very handy when it comes to writing. One of the many joys of writing for Rory is the range and quality of his impressions, giving us the opportunity to write for a particular voice. Indeed, certain impressions can suggest material unique to that individual, whether it's Rory's delightfully oily, creepy Michael Howard, resembling nothing so much as a smug vampire who's just been put in charge of the Blood Transfusion Service, or the simple realisation that Rory's take on William Hague's Yorkshire accent makes saying the word "Benghazi" simply hilarious. It's a remarkable gift that Rory has, and it's a gift to us as writers.

The BBC ask Rory to do an end of year special looking back over the year and we're asked to write for it. Spoiler alert, "No" win, 55.3% to 44.7% - on an astonishing 84.6% turnout, the highest for any UK election since 1910.

The last time Scotland witnessed a 90% turnout was the Highland Clearances.

This may be one of the riskiest jokes we've ever written and the fact that Rory uses it to a live Edinburgh audience is testament to his bravery as a performer and commitment to 'the joke'.

Figure 10: David Cameron campaigning in Scotland.

Was the voting age lowered to 16 to account for shorter life expectancy?

Cameron is so completely out of touch with Scotland and Scottish politics that he needed Gordon Brown as an interpreter, effectively. Pretty much how the entire British Empire was built. Tories with a brown native guide.

When Alex Salmond was talking about an independent Scotland being part of Europe, I think he may just have misunderstood how the Ryder Cup works.

Disappointed independence supporters take to wearing "45%" badges to indicate their continuing allegiance:

Wearing a "45%" badge is like tattooing "loser and proud of it" on your forehead.

There are nasty scenes in George Square in Glasgow after the results are announced, with Union Flag-waving Glasgow Rangers supporters to the fore, at a time when their team are languishing in the lower leagues following a financial scandal:

The team may not have made it back to the premiership yet, but Rangers' fans still lead the bigotry league…

For most of 2014, Rory is putting his talents in the hands of another writer, but we really don't mind as that writer is Noel Coward, and Rory is starring in a production of *Relative Values* which tours nationwide and then moves to the West End in the summer. We told you he's multi-talented. We keep our eyes on the political landscape while he's busy treading the boards.

Nationally, Nigel Farage's UKIP win an alarming 24 seats in the European elections in May, ironically elections they profoundly wished to abolish. The witches' brew that will spill over into Brexit gained another ingredient. Worryingly, the response to it on social media shows that the nature of political discourse is changing for the worse.

I find it rather sad that people seem more intent on insulting UKIP supporters rather than trying to understand why they feel that way and it's not good enough just to say they're 'racist' or 'stupid' - that's precisely the kind of lazy labelling that UKIP are attacked for.

Other seeds of future crises are being sown across the world. Russia hosts the Winter Olympics in Sochi – a Black Sea resort town where it never snows (and if that's not a metaphor for Putin's Russia, I don't know what is).

Russia then promptly gains international pariah status by invading the Crimean peninsula and other eastern areas of Ukraine, following highly questionable referenda. The pro-Russian government in Kyiv is overthrown by a popular, pro-EU revolution:

Can't we just exchange the Ukrainians who want to be part of the EU for UKIP? Putin can invade them all he likes.

Chapter Seven

A Rolling Edstone Gathers No Votes.

2015

("Rory Bremner's Election Report", BBC2, Tour/speaking engagements, 2015)

"Welsh rugby star George North says he's absolutely fine after suffering four concussions, and Brian, the giant talking daffodil that follows him everywhere, agrees."

You would be forgiven for feeling concussed yourself by the end of 2015, and if you think things will calm down in the years ahead, boy are you wrong. Hindsight's a bitch, ain't it? We've been hinting at some of the early precursors of Brexit but having reached 2015, we're at the real start of that particular tragicomedy, played out over three General Elections, a referendum, and something akin to (un)civil war in both major parties and to some extent the wider country.

The General Election is on May 7th and polling suggests that Labour and Conservative are evenly matched. The Coalition has been consistently unpopular (see all previous chapters of this book) and Labour is still locked in a furious identity crisis as it emerges from the Blair/Brown years when they actually, you know, *won* things, and won them a lot. In an apparent attempt to undo this disturbing trend, in 2010 the party had elected Ed

Miliband as leader rather than his Foreign Secretary, better-looking, more Blair-like and more likely to win brother David.

Nonetheless, Labour have a small lead in the polls as the campaign opens: surely all they have to do is not make any horrendous mistakes to return to government? Enter Miliband, Ed, apparently determined to prove that he is the worst brother since Cain. First there is the "Edstone", a £2.6m limestone tablet with various campaign pledges carved on it. Clearly the idea is that Labour's promises are 'carved in stone', but the hubris, comedy value and glaring impracticality of the thing – imagine the Laurel-and-Hardy-worth slap-stick of it being manhandled on and off the Election battle bus as it trundles up and down the country – dooms it from the start. It is instantly – and, being Twitter, we mean **instantly** - ridiculed. Boris Johnson describes it as "some weird Commie slab" and one Labour spin doctor is said to have started screaming at the television when it's unveiled:

The Edstone, the heaviest suicide note in history.

Look, it wasn't the Sun what won it this time, it was the brother that lost it.

The icing on Ed's bumper cake of failure is the resurfacing of a very odd photo, taken in 2014, of him eating a bacon sandwich, looking like, well, no one was quite sure, but normal human being" is a distant 100-1 shot with most bookmakers. *The Sun* have it on their front page the day before the election. If it was a Marmite sandwich it would be less divisive. Or better still, a marmalade one which he produces from under his red hat. Though if he wore a red hat he'd most likely be ridiculed for that too.

Figure 11 Ed Miliband sweeping up the smouldering remains of his political career.:

Meanwhile, David Cameron is, broadly speaking, acting like he doesn't think he has a chance in hell of winning and giddily promises all kinds of things in the belief he won't have to deliver on a single one of them.

Most significantly, in order to shore up support on the Tory Eurosceptic Right (THEM again!) and fend off the challenge of UKIP (also THEM again), he promises a substantive in-or-out referendum on the UK's membership of the EU.

Looking back, this now feels like that bit of a crap horror movie where the characters opt for a short cut through the spooky graveyard while the audience screams at them to just get a bloody Uber like normal people. Oh Mr Cameron, did you have to? We still haven't forgiven you. Neither have our kids, whose kids or grandkids will have to negotiate an odious, second-rate and grovelling treaty to get us back in.

Random thought, if Brexit is a horror movie, and let's be honest, it is, does that make Theresa May the Final Girl?

Talking of horror movies, let's get back to the General Election. On 7th May the variably-motivated electorate go to the ballot box. The final set of polls show Labour and Conservative neck and neck. Polling stations close at 10pm and the exit poll shows a Tory lead that, if it plays out, will, shockingly, give them an overall majority.

Former Lib Dem leader Paddy Ashdown is on the BBC's election coverage as a pundit and famously says he'll eat his hat if the exit poll proves correct. By the early hours of the morning, when it becomes apparent that it is in fact, correct, the BBC are asking Paddy whether he'd like fries with that. He doesn't eat it, of course.. Bloody politicians, never keep their promises- although when he appears on Question Time the following night he's given a marzipan hat to chow down on. Is there anything more British than trolling someone with cake?

Hats (uneaten) off to the Tories, though.

Shock ripples across social media – there'd been a big campaign to get younger voters to the polls, hoping their vote would put Labour in power. Unfortunately, not enough of them put their phones down for long enough to go and vote. Of course, it may be that they just found the electoral choices offered to them awful and dispiriting beyond words. For the statistically minded amongst you, here are the final scores:

Turnout 30.6 million (66.4%, up 1.3%)

	Votes	Vote Share	Seats
Conservative	11,334,726	36.9% (up 0.8%)	330 (up 24)
Labour	9,347,324	30.4 (up 1.5%)	232 (down 26)
SNP	1,454,436	4.7% (up 3.1%)	56 (up **50**)
Lib Dem	2,415, 862	7.9% (down 15.2%)	8 (down **49**)
UKIP	3,881,099	12.6% (up 9.5%)	1 (up 1)
Green	1,157,630	3.8% (up 2.8%)	1 (no change)

Meanwhile on Facebook:

YAY! DEMOCRACY! EVERYONE VOTE!

OH SHIT! BOO! DEMOCRACY! EVERYONE VOTED!

I HATE EVERYONE!

Cameron has a majority of twelve seats, helped in part by the fact that the SNP have won a landslide in Scotland, almost wiping out Labour north of the border in the process. His coalition partners, the Lib Dems, take a hammering, losing an astonishing 49 seats, being left with just 8. It's the most seats lost since the that time the DFS in our home town of Durham flooded.

Well, after last night, the Lib Dems can now reconnect with their past and call themselves the Gang of Eight. (The Social Democrats, precursors to the Lib Dems had been founded in 1981 by a "Gang of Four" disillusioned Labour MPs.)

Cameron:

I'm very relieved I'm not having to build another ghastly coalition. People said that I might have to get into bed with the Ulster Unionists, and I know they're not keen on that sort of thing. Very cold hands, I hear.

How did we win? Well, in keeping with our privatisation agenda, I've outsourced our unpopularity to the Lib Dems.

Labour, as ever, are one step behind us – we were wiped out in Scotland years ago and they've only just got round to it.

UK unemployment is at its lowest for seven years. Impressive, considering all those Lib Dem and Scottish Labour MPs now looking for jobs.

We in the Conservative party are all about supporting working families. Except the Milibands.

Cameron faces two significant realities: firstly, his majority is so small that he needs all his MPs, Eurosceptic right included, to vote with the government at all times in order to get anything done. Secondly, he now needs to deliver the EU referendum that he'd promised before the election to keep his party at least looking united, and his government able to push through legislation.

Over on the opposition benches, Ed Miliband resigns as Leader of The Labour Party and the "Edstone" is the subject of many a satirical eBay listing.

"For Sale: large limestone monolith, possible garden ornament or novelty kitchen worktop. Unfortunately, some idiot's carved incomprehensible nonsense on it. Opening bid £0.01. No reserve. Will deliver for a bacon sandwich."

David Miliband resigns as an MP and goes to run the International Rescue Committee, which is basically Thunderbirds, right? Cool. To date, he's doing an excellent job as Scott following a successful eyebrow transplant.

The leadership election rumbles on through the summer under a system that Ed Miliband (increasingly looking like a Tory sleeper agent bent on destroying Labour) has introduced, which gives the Unions a much greater say in choice of leader at the expense of the influence of the Parliamentary Party. This results in the election of longtime recalcitrant back bench rebel Jeremy Corbyn as leader in September, despite being supported by very few of the MPs he now leads. Never mind that the only things he'd led to date were rousing renditions of The Red Flag. Thinking musically, again we decide to mutilate a popular song:

The Corbyn Time Warp

It's just a jump to the left

Then a step to the left.

Put your hands on your hips

And be outraged at Tories

It's just the media lies

That drive you insa-a-a-ane

Let's lose the election again!

We also thought he might have trouble filling his cabinet, given his lack of support amongst MPs:

"Corbyn unveils 'unifying' top team'. Pretty sure 'Unifying' is missing an 'Ed' in the middle. Much, incredibly, like Labour is.

Latest shadow cabinet appointments.

Leader and Foreign Secretary: Jeremy Corbyn

Home office: Corbyn, J.

Treasury; John "Ronald" McDonald

Environment: Keir Hardie's cap.

Business: Trotsky's ghost.

Defence: Steptoe

DWP: and son.

Secretary of State for Northern Ireland: Gerry Adams

Corbyn is a polarising figure from day one. He's gained many supporters in the 18-25 age group by promising to scrap student loans, tax the rich and give all of them a free bong. We may have made that last one up. Festival crowds soon discover that they can chant "ohhhhh, Jer-em-y Cor-byn" to the tune of *Seven Nation Army* by The White Stripes, rapidly propelling it to the top of the most-annoying-cover-version charts, displacing longtime number one Jagger and Bowie's camp-as-a-field-full-of-chiffon-tents version of *Dancing in the Street*. Corbyn's anti-fans take to Twitter in droves. The peak of this is an account which automatically replies "F*ck off, Steptoe" to every tweet Jeremy makes.

More serious political criticism comes from the Blairite wing of the party who strongly feel that Corbyn simply cannot win an election. Labour had won three elections in a row under Blair by moving to the centre ground, where large parts of the electorate seemed most comfortable. Moving to the left had simply never worked at the ballot box. It also seems ridiculous that someone who had voted against the party whip over 300 times is now responsible for party discipline. Poacher turned gamekeeper doesn't even come close.

Then there's the IRA problem, something that Tim feels particularly keenly. At the height of the IRA's campaign in Northern Ireland (where Tim grew up), Corbyn had invited members of Sinn Fein to Westminster for tea and a photo op. Sinn Fein was little more than the political mouthpiece of the IRA at the time. It felt like an unforgiveable sin for many people. Tim's never got over it, possibly because he wasn't invited. Corbyn's number two, John McDonnell, held similar views to Jeremy.

Update from the Council on what to put out on the pavement for disposal and when:

Week 1: rubbish bin

Week 2: recycling bin.

Week 3: Corbyn.

During the election campaign, David Cameron claimed to be a West Ham supporter having previously said he supported Aston Villa, which led to us writing this silly joke:

John McDonnell accidentally says that he supports Aston Villa, not the IRA.

As events unfold, perhaps the most significant aspect of Corbyn's political beliefs is the fact that he is an instinctively and ideologically opposed to the EU which he regards as a "Bosses'" organisation. He had campaigned against the EU consistently and had written hundreds of speeches and articles on the subject all of which were on his personal website. Until every single one was deleted in early 2016.

Later in 2015, Hilary Clinton, perhaps inadvisably, describes Donald Trump's melange of supporters as a "basket of deplorables". If that is the case, the looming Brexit is filling its own basket: Farage, the Eurosceptic Tories, Corbyn. Surely such an unlikely coalition can't achieve anything? Surely? We've said that before.

The Rugby World Cup comes to the UK in the Autumn to cheer us up: Rory is asked to speak at a send-off dinner to wish the Scottish team good luck (they'll need it, sorry Rory!) and asks us to write some material:

I believe Nicola Sturgeon wants to change the Scottish Rugby Union's name to Scottish Rugby Independent within the European Union. Her proposal that in response to the New Zealand All Blacks' Haka, the Scottish team should dance onto to the pitch to the tune of 'Dashing White Sergeant' is unsubstantiated.

It's amazing, the influence of the British school system on sport: so there's Rugby, Eton Fives, and St Xaviers 100m Running Away from Father O'Donnell.

The Haka would be a lot less intimidating if the opposition held up scorecards for technical merit and artistic expression.

The Sun are sponsoring the England team to do the phonehaka.

I misunderstood about this being a Sendoff dinner so I only prepared 10 minutes of material.

Is a sin bin another name for Jonathan King's recycling?

We can be the Jeremy Corbyn of this World Cup. Enter for a laugh and end up winning it.

Try, try and try again. Is actually the All Blacks motto, strangely enough.

There's a clear message to be taken from the Labour Leadership Election for teams in this competition. They think they lost in the past because the ball didn't go right out to the left wing - even though they were very successful a few years ago running it straight down the middle.

Before you move on to the next chapter, we need to issue a very 2024 double trigger warning: it's basically all about Brexit **and** Trump. Sorry.

Chapter Eight

The Secret Diary of Nigel Farage, Aged 56 and ⅓

2015-16

(Breaking the News - BBC Scotland, various Tour/media appearances, December 2015 - July 2016).

"At this rate, the only thing left in the shadow cabinet will be shadows."

On 17th December 2015, Parliament passes an act that requiring that a referendum be held to determine whether the UK should remain part of the EU. The date of the referendum is set for 23rd June 2016.

Forty years have passed since the country voted 67-33% to join the EEC (as it was then). Ever since, elements of the Conservative party (and a small but loud minority on the Labour benches) have complained about it constantly and loudly. They are aided by a number of newspapers, notably the *Mail* and the *Express* who simply make stories up about the EU, normally to do with the banning of some British holy grail like sausages *"Hands off our bangers"* or bent bananas or just taking the piss out of the French. Many still think of Europe as being "over there" and that if geography hadn't seen fit to join us to the rest of the continent, politics shouldn't either. This is both geologically and historically ignorant, but when did that ever change anything? Sigh.

There had been intermittent crises such as the one over the Maastricht Treaty in 1992, which paved the way for the EU as it is today, with a common, if troubled, currency and an overarching EU citizenship. As usual, the Tory right threw up their hands in horror and led otherwise mild-mannered Prime Minister John Major to refer to three of his senior cabinet ministers as "bastards", believed to be Michael Howard, Peter Lilley and well known sartorially-challenged trainspotter Michael Portillo.

Were one so minded, one could frame the political history of the UK over the last 30 years as being *entirely* driven by that Tory Eurosceptic wing, and to a lesser extent, their Labour equivalents. The widespread – and entirely correct – perception of the Major government as being hopelessly and irrevocably split was one of the many, many factors that contributed to New Labour's 1997 monumental landslide election victory.

Back to 2015, and the referendum is the moment they've been waiting for to pollute the mainstream with their previously outlier beliefs. The issue has been forced by the rise of UKIP, a group led by Nigel Farage, full of people for whom the right-wing Tory Eurosceptics are neither right wing nor sceptical enough, astonishingly. If there was a silent movie melodrama version of Brexit, Farage would be the villain with top hat, cape and outrageous moustache, cackling as he ties poor Britannia to the train tracks.

The two campaigns are christened "Leave" and "Remain" making news bulletins sound like the practice ring at Crufts. Politicians from all sides align themselves according to their beliefs or, more likely, which one they think they will do better out of. Nominally, both the Government and the Labour Opposition line up on the Remain side, though of course many Tory MPs openly support Leave. Labour has the added problem of both an anti-European leader plus the knowledge that many of their traditional supporters in the post-industrial north are profoundly Eurosceptic. This is despite living in a region which has benefitted from literally billions of EU funding. Every other mainstream political party in the UK and in the Commonwealth, also support Remain. This allows the Leave side to portray themselves as rebels, sticking it to da man, to politicians out of touch with "ordinary people". Whoever they are.

Then there's Boris. Alexander Boris de Pfieffel-lookatmememEShopattesco-Bandwagonchaser-babydaddy Johnson.

Mary very memorably describes him as:

The secret lovechild of Donald Trump and Angela Merkel.

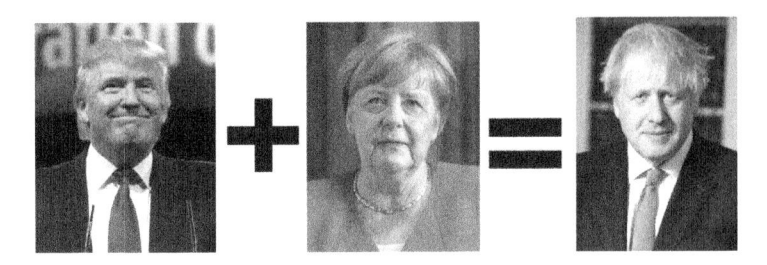

A joke which Rory uses repeatedly, including a memorable occasion at a dinner when Boris was one of the guests. History does not record whether he was amused, flattered or insulted (like we care). But then, what Boris thinks about anything is, to put it mildly, something of a moving target.

He becomes an MP for the second time in 2015 after two terms as London Mayor and is one of the leading voices calling for a referendum. Nonetheless, he seems to flirt with supporting Remain, writing two versions of an article for The Spectator, one of which will be published according to which way he jumps. We shouldn't be surprised, as flirting is, as we know, a particular hobby of his. Ahem. To no-one's real surprise he chooses Leave and becomes the unlikely poster boy for the campaign along with Nigel Farage, who looks more like a used car salesman with some dodgy bookmaking on the side every day. The two of them together make the campaign seem at times like an ill-advised and badly written reboot of *Minder*. Boris is also very fond of a catchy phrase:

Boris says that leaving the EU is "win-win". Funny, I thought that was the new panda in Edinburgh Zoo.

You put your left wing in, your right wing out, in-out-in-out and make it all about / border security, then you change your mind, because that's what it's all about.

So, the teams are set, just about the same time as the Six Nations Rugby is kicking off, and we have the opportunity to write for Rory's affectionately wonderful Bill McLaren impression:

We're underway in this opening fixture in the 28 Nations championship, Cameron at inside right kicks it off and it's taken by Johnson on the right wing, Duncan Smith throws him a dummy but he's plowing ahead and - oh my goodness, Johnson's running back towards his own team! He's jinking right and further right, and he's scored, right under the posts, and to celebrate he's drop-kicked Cameron through the uprights.

The campaign is by turns nasty, dull and surreal. Often all in the same day. A Leave battlebus emerges with "We give the EU £350M a week – let's fund our NHS instead"

Remember kids! The numbers on the bus aren't real £s, aren't real £s, aren't real £s…

The responses to this fall into four categories:

- It's an underestimate
- It's an overestimate
- It's a lie
- It's on a bus. LOL.

Michael Gove (Leave, inevitably, if you've been paying attention), when challenged with the fact that numerous economic experts have said that Brexit will be a disaster, responds to the interviewer by saying:

"We've had enough of experts".

This may be the most profoundly disturbing thing said by a British politician since George Galloway asked for some more Whiskas on Big Brother.

There's a genuinely horrifying degree of xenophobia or flat-out racism within the Leave campaign, wrapped up in talk of "controlling our borders". It is clear `that for some it isn't just about free movement in the EU. The perennial – and unquestionably racist - tabloid anxiety about "asylum seekers" has found a new legitimacy. Interestingly, some of the biggest Leave votes would be in areas with some of the lowest numbers of immigrants.

The Remain campaign focusses on the things we'll miss out on:

If we vote to leave the EU there'll be no more EUlogies, EUphemisms or EUphoniums. I'm still trying to work out if that's a bad thing.

The more serious concerns raised by Remain lead to them being characterised as "Project Fear" by the Leave campaign, trying to scare the poor British electorate into voting for them. It's interesting to note how Leave becomes ever more about feeling and less about facts, whereas Remain go the other way. It doesn't matter how much immigration there actually is, if you *feel* there's too much that's all that matters.

*Yes, sir, I know you **feel** that you're not having a heart attack. Do you want the bloody ambulance or not?*

From our point of view, it feels like are lots of reasons why people will vote one way or the other, which have nothing to do with our membership of the EU:

Reasons to Vote Leave

- *I hate the government*
- *I like Boris*
- *I like buses*
- *Gosh, isn't £350m a lot of money?*
- *Sausages*

Reasons to Vote Remain

- *I like the Government (unlikely, but there is probably someone)*
- *I hate Boris*
- *I don't like buses or the people who use them*
- *I've got a house in France*
- *Cheese*

The Pollsters, having messed up royally at the 2015 Election, show the two campaigns broadly neck and neck until the last couple of days before the vote on June 23rd, when they show Remain leading 52%-48%, within the margin of error.

All is set for the day of the vote. We know Rory will be in demand as a pundit once the results are out – but which jokes will we be writing?

Chapter Nine

The storm after the storm.

2016

(Miscellaneous Topical Material & Breaking the News June-August 2016.)

"...and now the weather. Widespread shitstorms with outbreaks of existential despair developing later."

At around 1:30 am on 24th June 2016 the first result comes in from those perennial counting overachievers, Sunderland. It's 61-39% Leave. Holy hell, we think. A leave vote was expected there but it is the margin that's a shock.

There's no exit poll as these are based on previous comparable elections, so we just have to wait anxiously to see what happens. As results come in, two things become clear: it is going to be very, very close and that there are striking divisions across the UK. Most of England has voted Leave, except London which votes strongly Remain. Scotland has voted overwhelmingly Remain, Wales shows a similar pattern to England. There is also a split on age, with the young voting overwhelmingly Remain, whilst older voters tend the other way. There is a lot of anger from young people who feel they'd been robbed of their futures of EU citizenship, gap years and 18-30 Holidays. By their grandpa and grandma. It feels very personal for many.

The nation wakes up to a 52-48 Leave victory (on a sort-of respectable-it'll-do 72% turnout) within the margin of polling error. Nigel Farage himself had previously said that if it was a 52-48 win for Remain "this wouldn't be over". Surely it's too close to act on? Isn't it just an advisory referendum? Seventeen million have voted to Leave – less than one third of the total UK population. The world's news cameras swing to number 10 Downing Street, and we write some jokes through our tears while we wait. As some form of therapy, if nothing else:

Tuesday. Entire UK wakes up from dreadful nightmare, phones EU to check we're still having that pizza on Friday.

Filled up with petrol on the way here. £2.50 a litre when I started, by the time I'd finished it was a tenner a gallon.

See someone looking confused outside their door? It's probably a Leave voter who didn't realise that voting to go out would mean they were out.

Nigel Farage: *<sings> you don't get me we're out of the Union. / I've won the Euromillions. Jackpot!!!*

What are we going to do now we're single? Go on match.com? "mature country, good sense of humour, own deterrent, theoretically solvent seeks partner for extravagant post-marital revenge trading".

We'll have to catch the very Cross-channel ferry from now on.

And then the door of Number ten opens: David Cameron emerges and resigns as Prime Minister on the spot:

Cameron: *I love this country, I love the British people. Well, except for seventeen million of you.*

I think it's a shame that many of our young people have vented their anger at the older generation. It's important that we cherish them, give them useful roles in society. School crossing patrols, leader of the opposition, that kind of thing.

I said I wanted to be the leader of a Conservative Party that wasn't always banging on about Europe. That hasn't gone too well but at least I don't have to do it anymore. Up yours, Boris, you fat lying bastard.

Poor Cameron. He'd won an election he thought he'd lose and lost a referendum he thought he'd win. Whatever happened to him? Oh yes, right. Fast forward to 2024, Peerage and Foreign Secretary.

Figure 12: Samantha Cameron waves goodbye to all those swine who voted Leave.

So what *has* happened? How on earth have we got to this point?

Both campaigns had been surprisingly lacklustre – Remain never seemed to understand that they needed to do more than simply say "It's Europe, right? Nice holidays, Eurotunnel, good chocolate, yeah?" (we're paraphrasing somewhat). Leave had shouted about borders and "taking back control" (whatever that meant) and pointed at a bus. Both sides had celebrity supporters whose contributions ranged from the poignant to the downright bizarre. Bob Geldof (Remain) traded insults with Nigel Farage (self-appointed CEO of Leave plc), boat-to-boat on the Thames over the likely effect of Brexit on the fishing industry. Geldof's boat was hosed down and boarded by angry fisherman and the famously calm and eloquent Irishman flicked the V's at Nigel. It all came across like some horrendously low budget theme park knock-off of *Pirates of the Caribbean*.

Remain singularly failed to target older voters by pointing out that there hadn't been a war in Europe since 1945 because countries that had spent the previous 1000 years fighting each other on and off were now part of a political and economic union. Peace paid a massive dividend since 1945 and no-one said it, and that was and is an utter, stupid bloody tragedy, not least because look, now there's a war in Ukraine. A proper land war in Europe, right bloody now.

GRRR.

Jeremy Corbyn had been nominally part of the Remain campaign but his office had turned down almost all requests to speak at or attend pro-Remain campaign events. Turmoil reigned in every party, even UKIP: when a single-issue party achieves its singular aim, what the hell does it do next?

It's safe to say that any of the political parties would like to be as beloved a British institution as *Gardeners' Question Time*:

Cameron : *I've got a lot of trouble with my grass roots. What can I do?*

To be honest, David, that is a tricky one. You can try spreading a lot of manure down there. A good spray of silage should do wonders.

Cameron*: That's the problem! They're full of it already.*

Corbyn*: I'm trying to prune my party of dead wood. Where should I start?*

You definitely need to start with the useless suckers that have grown right up from the base. They look good at first but they're always ultimately disappointing. Does that help?

Corbyn*: oh sorry, too late, it's all dead.*

Farage*: how do I go about getting rid of non-native plants from my garden?*

Well, what you need to do is go down to the garden shed, open the door, go in, and stay there. Hey presto, you can't see anything that bothers you now.

Farage*: I think there's an asylum seeker under the potting bench. Oh, no, it's the cat.*

So, what next? What will Brexit look like, how will it be achieved? Who it will it be achieved by is the first question to answer as, following David Cameron's resignation, an election process to choose the new Conservative leader, and thus the new Prime Minister begins. These are the runners and riders:

- Theresa "Darling Buds of" May
- Andrea "not born to" Leadsom

- Michael "Backstabber" Gove
- Stephen "who?" Crabb
- Liam "the NHS is as safe as a henhouse in my hands" Fox

A notable non-runner is Boris "Buffoon" Johnson, who was widely expected to put his name forward, with backing from Michael Gove. Gove announces his own candidacy (it's unclear whether Johnson knew about it in advance) which is a fatal blow to Johnson's campaign. He makes the decision to pull out, so there's a first time for everything.

Boris sings to Gove.

"I bet you're wondering how I knew

about your plan to be top blue

With some other guys you knew before,

Of all of the Tories you know I love you more

it took me by surprise I must say

when you announced it today,

oh-oh, I heard it through the Gove Vine"

Ironically, Gove's treachery pretty much dooms his campaign from day one. The Tories don't like a backstabber: many in the wider party still hadn't forgiven party grandee Michael Heseltine for his part in bringing down Margaret Thatcher 25 years ago.

After brief and largely uninteresting scuffles around Westminster, Tory MPs select Andrea Leadsom and Theresa May to go forward to a vote of grass roots Party members. Leadsom promptly withdraws and just like that Theresa May becomes Prime Minister. There's much grumbling on social media about the fact that she's become PM without a general election but they are largely shouted down by the those who've had more than enough of endless bloody elections.

Those people really aren't going to enjoy the next couple of years, are they? Never mind, eh?

International reactions to the Brexit vote vary widely – within the EU there is a good deal of sadness and pledges of continuing friendship. Right wing leaders, growing in popularity across the continent, welcome it as part of a far-right populist movement sweeping Europe. The UK, which had led the fight against rampant European nationalism in 1939-45 has become its unlikely champion. Another bloody tragedy.

Football is determined to outgun politics in the WTF stakes and do so when Leicester City win the Premier League. Reality has clearly lost the plot, and just in case you think it hasn't, Gary Lineker presents Match of the Day in his boxer shorts, as he'd promised to do if his former team Leicester won the league.

Many in the wider world clearly think, with no little sadness, that one of the world's oldest and most venerable democracies has lost its fricking mind. Thankfully, one of the other great democracies on the other side of the Atlantic is asking someone to hold its beer and is about to have its own psychotic breakdown and distract everyone. Yay.

Clue: it's *not* Canada.

Chapter Ten

Chronicle of a Trump Foretold.

2016

(Miscellaneous topical material/Breaking the News July-December 2016)

There's a poll showing that a third party or independent candidate could beat Trump and Clinton. For pity's sake no one tell George Galloway.

Long before it becomes a reality, the idea of Donald Trump being, or running for President has been the stuff of comedy. In 2000, the Simpsons famously predicted a Trump Presidency but they weren't the only ones. The Washington Post's famous comic strip *Doonesbury* regularly used Trump as a character and also played out a Trump presidential run around the same time as the Simpsons. Another syndicated strip, *Bloom County*, had Trump's brain being transplanted into a mangy, inebriated cat called Bill, one of the strip's regular characters, and then running for president – in **1987**.

We wondered what other sitcoms had unwittingly predicted future trends:

It Ain't Half Hot Mum (Global Warming)

Till Death Do Us Part (declining standards in the NHS)

On the Buses (Boris campaigns for Brexit)

Steptoe and son (The Labour Party)

Filthy Rich and Catflap (The European Research Group)

Whoops Apocalypse (Trump)

How can you write comedy about the reality of a thing when it already has a comic expression? Fortunately, Trump seems to be spiralling upwards in his egotism, narcissism and lack of any kind of brain to mouth filter. His reality **is** satirical.

Scene: it's 1997, cut to bathroom interior, Bill Clinton steps out of the shower. It's all been a dream. Fade to black.

Donald John Trump's story is well known, whether as embroidered by him in a torrent of gold-plated lies or told more accurately by his numerous biographers - one industry that the Trump Presidency undoubtedly boosts is publishing. Property developer, reality TV star, attempted nemesis to Barack Obama and friend of the rich and infamous, he is now the Republican nominee for President in the 2016 election. He's up against a woman whose life has seemed to lead to an inevitable peak as the first female President: Hilary Clinton, who probably already knew her way round the White House better than Trump did after his first term.

As he has done with US Presidents throughout his career, Rory quickly masters Trump's voice and mannerisms, and it will go on to be one of his most popular impressions as well as being an utter joy to write for.

Donelly the Elephant in the Room

To The USA

A political circus came

They brought a scary demagogue

And Donald was his name

On the right

They're all the bloody same

And off they run for the VP game

And are never seen again.

Ooooooooooooooooo....

tell the electorate

packs of lies and rumble

off to the White House

Nobody cares that you're a chump

Trump, Trump, Trump!

-

One by one, seemingly more likely candidates for the Republican nomination fall away, and the view of Trump as a possible President goes from "yeah, right" to "oh my god" via "surely not?". He tells clear, obvious and provably false lies, over and over again; but it becomes obvious that he is reaching the electorate on a massive scale. His message of "Make America Great Again" sells millions of red baseball caps but also resonates with a part of America that has felt left behind as traditional industries close and communities are ravaged by the exponentially growing opiate crisis.

Trump is an Internet comments section made flesh. Loud, angry and mostly wrong.

He certainly uses social media as no other politician has. His Twitter feed is an inflammable, explosive mix of lies, insults, grandstanding and invective, posted at all hours of the day and night, USUALLY ALL IN CAPITAL LETTERS. He coins the phrase "Fake News" - a catch-all cry (and hashtag) that tells his base to believe nothing except what **he** tells them. If he loses, he says, it will prove that the system is "RIGGED!". It is a new paradigm of propaganda for the twenty-first century and he is the absolute master of it. Anyone else saying the things he does on Twitter would be suspended but he brings millions of both followers and revenue to the platform and where Donald walks, money talks. His followers and fans love him and love how he makes them feel like they matter, like he understands them. He legitimises their anger, their confused bitter hatred of otherness. As demagogues always do.

He seems to get more orange every day, his red tie longer and longer, his hair more elaborate and gravity-defying, his supposed daily diet of Diet Coke and McDonalds fuelling his scattergun rages, and, one would assume, fuelling gusts of hot air from both ends.

It doesn't seem to matter what negative stories came out: whether it is the foul-mouthed on-tape confession of his abuse of women, or rumours swirling of links to Putin's Russia and its sprawling intelligence operations. Trump himself says he could shoot someone on Fifth Avenue and it wouldn't affect his support. No-one seems minded to disagree. He sells himself as an outsider who can go to Washington and "drain the swamp". Perhaps his most gobsmacking proposal is to build a wall between the US and Mexico to control the unchecked immigration his base are so worried about – and just to give it that extra twist of Trump's trademark craziness, he says he'll get Mexico to pay for it. Mexico, in polite, governmental, diplomatic language, tells him to go stuff himself.

Perhaps unsurprisingly, the one world leader who thinks it is a great idea is noted Israeli wall-fancier Benjamin Netanyahu.

Trump:

"We don't need no immigration
We just need more border control
No more brown children in the classroom
Teachers! Leave our guns alone!
Hey! Teachers! Leave our guns alone!
All in all we're just a bunch of pricks with a wall.
All in all we're just pricks with a wall."

The world seems to be building up a collection of "strong" male leaders, toxic masculinity expressed as neo-conservative political power: Trump, Boris, Farage, Erdogan and the original model of twenty-first century demagoguery himself - Vladimir Putin:

Paul Hollywood: *"Welcome to The Great Fascist Bake-Off! Tonight our four contestants are from the world of politics."*

First up to the bench is Nigel Farage.

Farage- *"I've baked a dessert for the Remainers - a hard cheesecake with sour grape topping. Actually I just bought the ingredients and left Boris to do it."*

Hollywood: *"Sounds like a recipe for disaster! I suppose there's no point in asking you to whip up a batch of brownies?*

Farage: *"Actually I can! I've got some in the back of the lorry."*

Boris: *"I'm making caught-shortbread. I had £350m worth of ingredients. Seem to have left them on the bus... I was hoping to get my hands on some of that EU butter mountain. Oh, hang on..."*

Hollywood: *"Fresh from his starring role on 'Make America Cake Again' here's Donald Trump."*

Donald - *"I'm going to bake a beautiful big white cake - the biggest you've ever seen - but MEXICO's going to pay for it."*

Hollywood: *"Wouldn't some fairy cakes be nicer?"*

Donald: *"Not if Mike Pence has his way! He's good at current buns. I like to grab myself a handful of hot tart."*

Hollywood: *"Only a handful? You on a diet? Hang on, can anyone smell smoke? Mr Putin?"*

Putin: *"Yes. Is Syrian Bombe Cake. Old Russian recipe."*

Hollywood: *"Another burnt offering from you, then."*

Putin: *"I used to have a problem with soggy bottoms - but I invaded the Crimea and its ALL FINE NOW! I've decorated my cake with an envelope full of cash. Please. Try it. And the cake. I'm told you like dough, boy..."*

Hollywood: *"Alright, alright. Keep your shirt on!"*

and so on…

We've always liked using an existing TV format as a 'tentpole' on which to hang material, whether it be the Bake Off, I'm a Celebrity, or the nations favourite Saturday night glitter-and-fake-tan fest:

Coming up tonight on Strictly C*nts Dancing, we have:

Nigel Farage performs the Independance with 17 million backing dancers

Donald Trump dances the American Schmooze partnered by his favourite person - himself

Boris Johnson gets into fancy dress as a serious politician and does the Birdie Dance partnered by whichever mother of one of his children he's with this week.

Michael Gove will be performing a Quickstab with the exhumed corpse of Margaret Thatcher – sorry Michael, it's the Halloween special next week!

And finally, Vlad Putin will be dancing all the way to Damascus with his partners Pestilence, War, Famine and Death!

Who will be in the bottom two? Who will have the Judges arrested? Will Donald's fake tan melt? Will World War III break out and tan everyone permanently? Stay tuned!

As the Presidential election campaign gets into full swing, Trump goes into overdrive. He christens his opponent "Crooked Hilary" and leads rally after rally in the chant of "Lock Her Up!". A row breaks out over Hilary's use of a private email server when she was Secretary of State under Obama. It's a non-story in many ways but Trump leaps on it as proof of her "crookedness". In a July news conference Trump asks Russia "if you're listening, can you find the 30,000 missing emails?". Typical Trump bluster, but it emerges that in the days following, Russia **does** attempt to hack into several Clinton-associated addresses. In some ways, it's much scarier if some of the awful things Trump says are true: it's easier and more sanity-preserving to assume they are all lies.

Here is the cock, the Trumpland cock, telling the lies steadily, crazily, never too quietly, never too dumbly. Telling the lies for Trumpland

Meanwhile Hilary, the embodiment of the American political establishment, is running a proper, conventional presidential campaign. In comparison to the Trump Circus, it is unbelievably, achingly *dull*. When she tries to up the ante – as when she refers to Trump's supporters as "a basket of deplorables" - it backfires on her. The email server story rumbles on, and on, likely with Russian intervention.

The idea that he might actually win begins to stalk Democrat and media nightmares – Trump calls the mainstream media "the enemy of the people", a hauntingly fascist echo. It's Hilary's time. Isn't it? Have they inadvertently selected the one candidate that can't beat Trump? Clinton is a pretty polarising candidate herself and she undoubtedly comes across as entitled, the latest member of the Bush/Clinton gang that have dominated the White House for much of the previous thirty years.

I've had a really nasty virus for nearly a week now, despite everything I've tried it just won't feck off. I'm calling it Donald.

November 8th 2016, Election day.

Something that seems to be both unbelievable and inevitable happens. He wins.

	Popular vote	*%*	*Electoral College*
Trump/Pence	62,984,828	46.1	304
Clinton/Kaine	65,853,514	48.2	227

It's worth noting that Trump had, at various times in his life, railed against the Electoral College system. He is suddenly a big fan. For now.

First we had Brexit.

Now Trump.

In the name of all that's holy, what the blinking flippity-flip is going on?

Chapter Eleven

The Darling Duds of May.

2017

(Breaking the News/The News Quiz/Tour, February-July 2017)

"How is it that people have only just noticed that the DUP are a bunch of reactionary nutters? It's like when the neighbours of a serial killer say "oooh, well, he was just a bit quiet, really, apart from laying a new patio every week."

If Donald Trump's rise to power feels like two demented circuses crashing into each other at 100mph, Theresa May's path to Number 10 seems more like a low-speed shunt not worth losing your no-claims bonus over.

She's an unlikely shepherdess to guide Brexit to something resembling a conclusion. She'd been firmly in the Remain camp, had been a regular figure in the shadow cabinet since 1999 and was rewarded by David Cameron with the post of Home Secretary in 2010, a post she held until her election as leader. She's the closest thing to a centrist in the contemporary party and her first speech as PM sounds positively Blairite at times. It represents an attempt to park herself in the centre ground of British politics, which has become an utter vacuum as both main parties seem under the control of their ideological outer limits.

A small historical note: Theresa's capture of Number Ten makes a prophet of Rod Stewart, whose 1971 classic 'Maggie May' turns out to be a Nostradamus-like prediction of the UK's first two female Prime Ministers. Her first cabinet is a broad mix of the party, but with arch Brexiteers in key roles: Liam Fox at Trade, David Davis as the newly created 'Minister for Leaving the European Union'. Snappy. On the top of the Brexiteer pile is Boris Johnson as Foreign Secretary, determined to be a flag-waving ambassador for a post-Brexit "Global Britain". He becomes the central hate-figure for depressed Remainers. His would-be assassin Michael Gove is consigned to the back benches for being such a naughty, naughty boy.

May-ry, May-ry, quite conservative,

How does your Brexit grow?

With silver heels and cock-up bills

And a shitty pest in the FO.

Samantha Cameron on the Bake Off, Ed Balls on Strictly, please, PLEASE can we send Boris to the jungle now?

> **Dec**: *So, Boris has been voted to do the bush tucker trial for a record 17th time in a row.*
>
> **Ant**: *That's right, Dec. It's a toughie tonight, he'll be trying to swallow the consequences of Brexit and failing miserably.*

May's unenviable first task is to decide exactly how to turn the referendum result into the UK actually leaving the EU. It is clear that whatever she comes up with, a lot of people (including in her own party) will utterly hate it and despise her personally for producing it. There are also legal challenges to the legitimacy of the referendum result beginning to pile up in the courts.

Newsreader: *a possible Brexit route map the prime minister could be preparing to follow is emerging.*

In other words, she's possibly thinking about planning to have a good think about planning to decide to start thinking about it. Possibly.

To May's badly concealed annoyance, the House of Lords is becoming very adept at frustrating Brexit legislation:

We have the unedifying spectacle of an unelected Prime Minister being defied by an unelected House of Lords. Rather appropriate, in some ways, when a vote by less than a third of the population apparently counts as the "will of the British people".

Thankfully, Brexit isn't the only game in town. Jeremy Hunt is still Health Secretary and has redrafted and imposed new contracts for junior doctors in the NHS, which is predictably unpopular:

Doctor Foster went to Gloucester,

Treating a lot of pain

His contract a muddle ,

His hours a fiddle,

So Jeremy wrote it again.

Boris: *Junior doctors, or Hunt saboteurs as I call them - they complain about working a 100-hour week, but they should be thankful - for each of them there are ten people on zero hours contracts who would love that many hours a month.*

In his new role as Foreign Secretary, Boris pays a visit to his "comedy daddy" Trump, who has generated howls of outrage after issuing an executive order banning immigration from six majority Muslim countries. It is finally overturned by the Supreme Court in June, to Trump's predictable fury. However, they do let Boris in and the two men clearly find a good deal of common ground: Trump speaks approvingly of the Brexit vote, and there is much talk of a renewed "special relationship":

What kind of special relationship is this, foreign secretary?

Boris: *well, well, I like to think of it as a very modern and open marriage, we say, yes dear, yes dear, and then do what we like. Having our own, own, um, policies, striking out on our own, having, if you like, a political child outside the marriage.*

Trump: *I heard a Boris was coming to see me and I remembered about the deal, such a good deal, that I made with Russia.*

Did you know that Boris' great, great grandfather was called Ali Kemal? Wonder if that'll come up next time he flies to America?

Boris has two of everything, two passports, two opinions on Brexit, two feet to stick in his mouth.

Of course, as he was born in the USA, he could be president. Astonishing to think that could be an improvement.

It's a IKEA flat pack Presidency: funny name, strange colour, screws missing.

As writers, we are secretly glad that Boris is Foreign Secretary. Rory has never 'done' female voices, feeling that there are plenty of excellent female impressionists around and they should be the ones to do those voices. Sure enough, the splendid Jan Ravens has rapidly nailed her Theresa May and is using it to great effect on BBC Radio 4's Dead Ringers.

After much shilly-shallying and many rowdy sessions in the Commons, the Article 50 letter is delivered to Brussels on 29th March and the process of leaving actually begins.

Remember, the clocks go forward tonight. And then back forty years on the 29th.

The delivery of Theresa's article 50 letter is notable in a number of ways – one of which is that it is a physical, hand delivered letter. And almost uniquely, the EU were actually in the first time we tried to deliver it. Giant red rubber band found outside EU secretariat in Brussels.

To keep the leave voters happy - not that that's possible - article 50 will now be officially renamed article 52%

Are the Leavers just jealous because Remoaners have multiple orgasms?

Well, we need to do something to cheer ourselves up.

The Prime Minister is clearly bothered by her lack of an electoral mandate and frustrated by various delaying tactics employed by determined Remainers. There is consistent criticism that something as significant as Brexit should be led by a Prime Minister with clear popular support. Remainers, on the other hand, hope that an early election can also be made into a *de facto* second referendum. On 19th April, Theresa May calls a snap election for June 8th.

April: May picks June.

There is something of a collective groan from an electorate suffering from PESD (Post Election Stress Disorder), exemplified by a vox pop from "Brenda in Bristol" who, when told that there is going to be another election, says, in a broad Bristol accent:

"You're joking! Not another one!"

Indeed, Brenda, another one. Sorry.

Once it begins, the election campaign is lacklustre. Neither of the main parties seem ready for it and we suspect that there are more than a few "Brendas" in both main parties, victims of CFS (campaign fatigue syndrome).

This campaign is the political equivalent of an episode of Pointless, with both parties apparently trying to produce policies that appeal to the fewest people possible.

There is **no** possibility of it becoming a vote on Brexit as both main parties remain (sorry) committed to implementing the result of the referendum, the bastards. The only party to offer an alternative is the Lib Dems but they seem to still be electorally toxic for many and continue to suffer from the "wasted vote" mindset. Nonetheless:

If you are angry about #Brexit and don't vote Lib Dem on June 8th, be prepared to shut the hell up for a few years. There is no nuance here.

Many in the Remain camp (sitting in authentic imported Mongolian yurts, naturally) still have a profound sense of personal loss:

The 5 stages of Brexit grief:

- **Denial**. *They won't do what Boris says.*
- **Anger**. *They did what Boris said?*
- **Bargaining**. *Ok, just don't give Boris an important job.*
- **Depression**. *Foreign Secretary. Oh, for feck's sake. I give up.*
- **Acceptance**. *Oh well. Might as well vote for Theresa.*

How do we make sense of this election? What is really at stake? It's in many ways an odd one, with the extreme views of UKIP defining the mainstream battlegrounds of the campaign. The truth is that no party can be confident about how Brexit will affect their policies and plans because we don't know what Brexit is.

This election is like buying a plane ticket without knowing where you are going, what airport you're landing at or what you're going to do when you get there. And what are we doing now? Arguing about the inflight meals. Yes, basically the UK is about to fly Ryanair, with oversized baggage.

Captain Theresa at the controls, Chief Steward Boris in charge of safety while diversity hire Jeremy is trying to persuade a member of Momentum in row R to hijack the plane together like they hijacked the party.

Indeed. Sure enough, a ho-hum campaign combined with a disheartened electorate produces an equally ho-hum result, despite a fractional increase in turnout:

Turnout: 32,204,184 (68.8%, up 2.4%)

	Votes	*Vote Share*	*Seats*
Conservative	13,636,684	42.3% (up 5.5%)	318 (down 13)
Labour	12,877,918	40% (up 9.6%)	262 (up 30)
SNP	977,568	3% (down 1.7%)	35 (down 21)
Lib Dem	2,371,861	7.4% (down 0.5%)	12 (up 4)
UKIP	594,068	1.8% (down 10.8%)	0 (down 1)
Green	525,665	1.6% (down 2.1%)	1 (no change)

Labour gain seats, but not enough, the Tories lose seats but not too many, the Lib Dems' pro-Remain stance nets them a whopping… four more seats. Leader Tim Farron resigns, presumably in disgust. He's replaced by Sir Vince Cable, who surprises many people by being;

> A) *Alive*
> B) *Not a Tory after all.*

Labour had problems during the campaign: Jeremy Corbyn seemed remarkably unwilling to say he wanted to be Prime

Minister. Which is a bit odd (and indeed a bit useless) if you're the leader of the Opposition. Shadow Home Secretary Diane Abbot had several car-crash interviews in which she repeatedly got various numbers and costs wrong or changed her mind mid-interview:

*Corbyn still can't say that he wants to be PM. Could this be because - shock horror - he actually doesn't want to be? He's been in opposition his entire life, even when Labour **were** in power he was in opposition to the government.*

I've just invented Diane Abbot bingo, in which someone shouts out random numbers that no one has on their card.

Seriously, how have Labour now managed to lose two elections against massively unpopular governments in a row? Incompetent doesn't come close. They couldn't organise an anti-Israel piss-up in a co-operative vegan brewery.

As in 2010, there's a hung Parliament, with the Tories as the largest party in search of coalition partners. The Lib Dems aren't interested so Theresa's glance goes across the Irish Sea to Northern Ireland, where the Democratic Unionists (DUP) have ten seats, just enough to give May a working majority. May and DUP leader Arlene Phillips eventually sign a "confidence and supply" agreement. This is all fine and dandy, except that the DUP really aren't very nice. Basically imagine the Taliban in bad suits, socially conservative, anti-LGBT rights. You get the idea. Having grown up with the DUP and their foul ilk, Tim is:

…most amused by the fact that for the first time in 30 years people on the mainland have finally noticed or cared what fecking nutters the DUP are.

I like the way Theresa is challenging Corbyn to a "who can have the most objectionable Northern Irish mates" competition.

It's amazing how ignorant most people in the U.K. were about the DUP. They think Orange Order is how you get a new phone.

Apparently the DUP did invite Trump to join the Orange Order but the Oompaloompas vetoed it.

It's only July and 2017 is already utterly exhausting. It's time to take a break and have a nice cup of Covfefe.

Chapter Twelve

140 characters and one very big one.

2017

(The Imitation Game, ITV; Breaking the News; Tour: July-December 2017.)

"Did Trump pull out of the Paris Accords because he thinks they're Japanese cars?"

Donald Trump and Twitter continues to be one of those perfect combinations: apple pie and ice cream; burger and fries; sado- and masochism. He's taken to its punchy 140-character format and sees it as the perfect way to disseminate simple, powerful, entirely untrue messages, completely lacking in nuance, grammar or any kind of moral compass whatsoever. So we get "Make America Great Again!" or "LOCK HER UP!" or any number of tweets condemning his opponents, members of his own party or the mainstream media, one of his favourite targets:

"I am thinking about changing the name of #FakeNews CNN to #FraudNewsCNN!"

To be fair, if CNN thought that might increase their dwindling viewing figures, they may have done just that.

Of course there are many much, much worse of Donald's tweets that don't require or merit repetition. Except for one. You know what's coming, don't you? Oh yes. On 31st May, 2017, just after midnight Dyslexia J Trump breaks the internet:

@realDonaldTrump: "Despite the constant negative press covfefe"

The #covfefe hashtag is used fourteen million times in the 24 hours following the tweet. Nobody cares what he had meant to type (let's be honest, we all know it's "coverage", but who cares?) and everyone takes it to mean whatever suits them. Democrats call it yet further evidence of mental decline. QAnon conspiracy cultists believe it is a coded message to them and set about trying to divine its *"real"* meaning. To be fair they do this with all his tweets: one theory holds that the tweets in ALL CAPS have special significance. We go down the acronym route:

> *Challenge Odd Visitors! Foreign Enemies! Feck Everything!*
>
> *Coke Only Vital, Food Eaten: Frankfurters. Easy.*
>
> *Count Our Votes, Forget Everything, Fraud Everywhere!*

That last one is oddly predictive of how Trump will behave after he loses the 2020 election (spoiler alert)…

And, also, with hindsight:

COVid. FEar! FEar!

Back to 2017, and Trump is indulging in some alarming nuclear sabre rattling with pariah state North Korea and its Pokemon-gone-bad leader Kim Il Sung. North Korea has longstanding nuclear ambitions continues to carry out tests of both the bombs themselves and also of increasingly long-range missiles. One recent test missile landed in the sea of Japan after flying through Japanese airspace. The Japanese, with better reason than anyone to be just a tiny bit twitchy about the whole nuclear weapons thing, are massively pissed off, though they probably expressed it more diplomatically. Or perhaps not. Kim's primary backer is China who like having a geographic and political buffer between them and South Korea, with its large, permanent US military presence, KFCs and Coke bottling plants. Without Chinese political, economic and military support the North Korean state would simply collapse. This allows China to be a restraining force on the North too, and is publicly so after Pyongyang tests its first Intercontinental Ballistic Missile (ICBM) in July. ("Bad Kim! You really do put the dick into Dictator")

Trump has already ordered a large-scale missile strike in Syria following use of chemical weapons by the Assad regime against civilians, so when he threatens North Korea with "fire and fury like the world's never seen" there is an unpleasant reminder that perhaps Trump's teeny tiny finger isn't really the one we want on the nuclear button, or indeed in the same building as it.

Now on BBC1, the fiery and furious everyday story of the North Korean Kim family as they race towards World War Three. Yes it's Far Eastenders!

We have a new Cold War with an aggressive US President, a female Tory PM and a useless left wing Labour leader. In other news, it's 1984 and I might be late for school and someone's stolen the knockoff Walkman I got from Dixons.

It's fair to say that given the amount of Diet Coke he drinks, Trump could probably be classed as a chemical weapon too. Perhaps even a Weapon of Mass Eruption.

Trump's foreign policy really doesn't make much sense. Shocking, I know. He pulls out of the Paris Accords on climate change and cancels America's membership of the World Health Organisation (WHO) – and boy, was that a decision with a strikingly short shelf-life. He also berates NATO members for 'not paying their share'. All whilst lobbing cruise missiles into Syria, threatening war on the Korean peninsula and cosying up to Putin, the leader of the country NATO was formed to defend against.

It's his relationship with the least popular Vlad since the Impaler, Russian de facto dictator Vladimir Putin, that is particularly odd and indeed troubling. Persuasive and continual rumours of Russian meddling in the 2016 Presidential election aren't going away, eventually leading to the appointment of a Special Counsel to investigate the links between Russia and the Trump campaign. To no-one's surprise, they find plenty, a view shared by both the FBI and CIA. Trump only avoids an obstruction of justice indictment as a sitting President can't be indicted. Once he isn't president, of course, he can be indicted on numerous grounds.

Trump's White House makes House of Cards look like the fecking Waltons.

In 2018, Trump and Putin meet in Helsinki for summit talks. They have two hours of secret talks at which only their interpreters are present and no notes are taken.

Take a minute and read that again.

It's hard to overstate how unprecedented this is. It's more like a handler debriefing his agent than a meeting of Heads of State and if that sounds like hyperbole remember that Vlad is ex-KGB. Trump emerges to say that he asked Vlad if he'd interfered in the election and Vlad said no so…cased closed. Contradicting his own intelligence community's official and unanimous view. Jeez Louise.

So, Trump asked Vlad if he did the thing that everyone knows he did, and Vlad said no, I didn't, and Trump told everyone who knew that he did it too that neither he or Vlad did the thing that everyone knows they did. So that's cleared that up.

A huge late winter snowstorm blankets much of North America in March, precisely the kind of dramatic weather events scientists warn will become more common due to climate change. Trump, the arch Climate Sceptic – he'd dismissed it as a "Chinese hoax" - leaps on it to say "so much for Global Warming!", and lots and lots of people agree with him, because for them he has bought off the biggest lie of all: that he, big fat fibber that he is, can be trusted.

Amongst his supporters are members of some deeply unpleasant far right groups and they feel legitimised by Trump's election and by the fact that he often retweets frankly appalling, racist, antisemitic things. Rumours abound that Melania gave him a book of Hitler's speeches for his birthday, which he keeps by his bed. If you think he is able to read words of more than two syllables, it could be true. Maybe he uses it to stir himself into action between the sheets.

In August, a tiki torch-carrying far-right protest clashes violently with anti-fascist protesters in Charlottesville, South Carolina. A car is driven into the crowd at one point and one of the antifascist protesters is tragically killed. Asked to comment, Trump condemns the violence but infamously says that there are "good people on both sides. On both sides". For many this is an unacceptable stance:

The problem with Trump's stance is that it's usually feet well apart, knees bent, ball slightly behind the left heel. Trump's obsession with golf explains a lot about his presidency: wearing terrible clothes, well below par and frequently in his bunker.

Yes, there was blame on both sides. Left and right. Sides of Trump's brain.

It's just a Trump to the left, then a Trump to the right, put your hands on your phone, and tweet all night. Let's do the news-warp again....!

All living former Presidents condemn him but it isn't their approval he wants. He has the far right vote sewn up like a white bedsheet. Or a body bag.

Trump's so ignorant about Nazis, he thinks 'Deutschland Uber Alles' is a German taxi firm.

More drama comes for Trump's Twitter: in November 2017, his account is taken down for eleven minutes by a "rogue employee" (Trump's description, that rules out almost none of his employees). We speculated about what things you could do in those Trumpless moments.

Outlast Boris' attention span by 10 minutes and 50 seconds.

Watch 15 celebrity careers go down in flames.

The 11 minutes Trump couldn't tweet really did make America great again. For 11 minutes.

You could have several cups of covfefe.

Cook 11 minute steaks. Or "breakfast" as Trump supporters call it.

Practice the four minute warning almost 3 times. You never know.

Alastair Campbell has said he was sure it was 45 minutes. Diane Abbot was unavailable for comment.

Trump has rapidly become our favourite voice to write for. His unique delivery is a swirling mess of mannerisms and vocal and physical tics. Rory masters them all and we're always on the lookout for new ways to use the impression. Trump begins to use language about immigration, jews and enemies foreign and domestic and Tim wonders how close to the language of the 1930's it is. The test: a routine called "Trump or Hitler", plans for Rory to deliver a set of lines as Trump, the lines being half Trump originals and half by Adolf Hitler. Not knowing quite how it will turn out, we do our research. The result goes something like this:

1. *"The ultimate goal must definitely be the removal of the foreigners altogether"*
2. *"You wouldn't believe how bad these people are. They aren't people. These are animals."*
3. *"If I don't get elected, it's going to be a bloodbath for the country"*

4. *"We must care for the purity of our blood by eliminating foreigners."*
5. *"Foreigners are poisoning the blood of our country."*
6. *"I am acting in accordance with the will of the Almighty Creator"*
7. *"God wants me to be President"*
8. *"These foreigners are rapists and criminals"*
9. *"Humanitarianism is the expression of stupidity and cowardice."*

(1,4,6 and 9 are Hitler, the rest Trump)

However, there's a problem. It's not really funny. It's too shocking, too downright terrifying to turn into a 2-minute comedy routine. There is no other way of making the same point – or perhaps it has to wait until we have the time to give it context. This happens sometimes: there's a story that catches our attention but it's too big, too dark. Of course, there are occasions when the darker stories make for satire that is just dangerous enough. There's a lot of talk in comedy and comic writing about 'the line', that hypothetical line that crosses from good comedy to bad taste. Some comedians like Frankie Boyle and Jimmy Carr have made careers straddling that line or indeed operating entirely beyond it.

We've often found that the best jokes approach the line then *just* pull back from it at the last moment. They can make an audience gasp and then immediately laugh. Tim's humour is particularly like this and it's a product of growing up during The Troubles, where humour was a vital defence mechanism against the insanities of that place and time. Mary's humour is sillier, more playful, with a keen sense of the absurd: we think it's why we write well together. We bring different things to the table/Word document.

Meanwhile, back in the UK, things around the Brexit negotiating table are *much* less harmonious…

Chapter Thirteen

Malcontents may have settled during transit.

2017

(The Imitation Game - ITV; Various Tour venues, July-December 2017.)

'Tory MP asks question at Prime Minister's Questions re: vocational education. Translation: "what will we do when all the Polish plumbers leave?"'

Emboldened by an election victory that surely must have surprised even her, and buttressed by the very loose cannons (and Canons) of the DUP, Theresa May sets about reshaping her cabinet to pull off yet another escape act: leaving the EU. All of the big guns stay in post in the reshuffle, giving the whole thing a business-as-usual vibe.

Where did Theresa get her latest shuffle from? Her iPod? Would explain why we've got Little Mix in the whips' office now.

Theresa May has vowed to get rid of "useless plastic waste". I thought the reshuffle was last week?

Labour, meanwhile, seem to be acting like they have won (which they should have) and don't change policy (which they should) or leadership (which they definitely should). Losing while attaining some kind of self-judged moral high ground seems enough for many within the party, and the three elections they'd won under

Blair seem to be something the party wants to forget if not actually positively disown. The truth is that they are every bit as split as the Tories on Europe, particularly in their traditional northern heartlands, the so-called Red Wall, something that will cause them to lose yet another election in 2019. There seem to be two Labour parties: the North and the North London. The upshot of all this is that it looks like Brexit really is going to happen, for all Theresa's talk about a "transition phase". FFS, thinks everyone else.

In other news and for those requiring distraction from such dispiriting realties (ie most of us), Love Island is on:

Tonight on Love Island – Theresa wants to break up with Claude but wants a transition phase while she pretends she still likes him. Jeremy tells Diane he wants to be the one that counts in her life, and god knows someone needs to - and Boris still can't make up his mind who he wants, what he wants or who he is. If you're not totally sick of voting, visit itv.com/loveisland.

North of the border, there's a lot of disquiet about Brexit. The country had voted overwhelmingly Remain and for remain-supporting parties in the General Election. Nicola Sturgeon is pushing the idea of an Independent Scotland that could rejoin the EU, and dreaming of Indyref2.

So we have a party leader greatly weakened by defeat in a referendum they expected to win, and then there's Theresa May.

The UK proposes a post-Brexit customs union which looks very much like being in the EU without being in the EU: Nicola (amongst many others, is dismissive):

Nicola Sturgeon has said that it's a 'daft have-cake-and-eat-it approach.' To be fair, that is the point of cake. What's the point of Nicola, again?

And so the country settles down into a normal British summer, alternately complaining about it being either too hot or too wet, sometimes simultaneously. For two whole months, there's nothing to vote for except Love Island and whose turn it is to clean the barbeque. Brenda from Bristol relaxes, as do political journos who probably hadn't slept much in the previous fourteen months.

In August the Duke of Edinburgh retires from public life, which is a shame as we'd got a lot of material out of him over the years. We'd always suspected that he was privately a very funny man indeed and treated his public appearances as an extended practical joke played on the media. We get one final celebratory line out of him:

Breaking: Prince Phillip retires to spend less time with his family.

Party Conference season rolls round in September and the Labour Party take ignoring the elephant in the room to the level of performance art by not having a single debate or motion about Brexit. None. Nada. Zilch. Zero. While their physical location (Brighton) is not in doubt, where they really stand on Brexit is anyone's guess. It's almost as if they think that by saying nothing, it can look like they agree with everyone.

Fortunately for them, the Tories outdo them with a Conference that is by turns baffling, controversial and outrageous. And that's just Boris Johnson, whose lowest moment comes when he tells a fringe meeting that Libya would be a great tourist destination "when they've cleared all the bodies away". It is, of course, filmed on multiple mobile phones and in the hands of the media before the meeting has finished. It's amazing how slowly politicians have grasped the new reality that everything, **everything** is filmed, recorded and screen-grabbed. If "Off the record" ever meant anything it means very, very little now. Everyone is a paparazzi, every unscripted remark a minefield.

Boris defends himself by saying that 'jokes can be "a very effective way of getting your diplomatic message across".

Which is presumably why Theresa gave him the job. Ha. Ha. Ha.

Apparently Bismarck was a noted practical joker, Sir Geoffrey Howe employed Ronnie Corbett as a speechwriter and Boutros-Boutros Ghali did a hilarious impression of Nelson Mandela at a meeting of the UN Security Council.

The Conservative Party need a barnstorming speech from the Prime Minister to end the conference on a high. It doesn't get one. Between coughing fits and being presented with a P45 by a protester, it resembles a cross between a below-par student revue and an advertisement for throat lozenges. It does, perhaps, make people feel sorry for Theresa, just a little bit, and Boris's travails mean she's likely to stay in post for a while.

Which is probably why we really ought to feel sorry for her. It doesn't last.

The "EU Withdrawal Bill" is passed in the House of Commons and spends the next ten months shuttling between the Commons and the Lords as their Lord- and Ladyships make a glorious ceremonial pain in the backside of themselves to the government. They become unlikely heroes to the increasingly glum Remainers: finally someone is doing *something*, even if in the end it won't make any difference. Whispers of the idea of a second referendum on the actual deal, when it is finally ready, began to circulate. This makes a lot of sense, as it is obvious to many that the original referendum only discussed whether to leave or not, not what the reality of leaving would be like.

It makes so much sense, in fact, that there is absolutely no chance on God's earth of it happening. Welcome to Brexit, twinned with the Upside Down from *Stranger Things*.

Of course, making the original question simple was the whole point: it allowed anyone to make Brexit what they wanted it to be about: for fisherman it was about ending hated EU quotas, for Nigel Farage it was about becoming famous enough to earn his living doing media appearances and for farmers – well, this was the funny one. It was completely insane for any farmer to vote for Brexit since it was apparent from day one that they were the one group who, thanks to a loss of EU subsidies paid under the Common Agricultural Policy, would be utterly screwed by Brexit. Yet some of them did. Wibble.

In an attempt to make it look like we're being consulted, David Davies, the minister for Leaving the EU, "concedes" that parliament will have an opportunity to vote on the specifics of the deal (whatever they are) once it is in place (whenever that is) and that this will obviate the need for a second referendum (bollocks will it). It's unclear what will happen in the event that Parliament vote against the deal and whether ministers will be willing to renegotiate the deal in that event (of course they won't).

This proves to be a mistake: in December a group of Tory rebels from the centre-left of the party hand the government its first significant defeat on Brexit by supporting a motion to give Parliament a meaningful and binding vote on the eventual deal. The EU rule that any transition period for the UK must end by 31st December 2020 at the very latest. The cliff is a little way away but it does still feel like the UK is intent on recreating the finale of *Thelma and Louise*. The reality is that the best we can hope for is the end of *The Italian Job* instead.

Happy Christmas, everyone. Except you, Nigel.

Chapter Fourteen

Easy answers, and other really difficult things.

2012 – present day.

Nuance – an interlude

Remember *nuance*? Yes? The idea that the best answer to most questions is almost never as simple as yes or no, in or out, Leave or Remain. It also encourages us to recognise that no viewpoint is utterly without merit, and to remember that it's certainly valid to the person who holds that view. That the things we have in common as human beings sharing this small planet matter more than the things that divide us. Philosophers like Hume, Rousseau, Plato , Marx and Sting have all said as much in their own way.

Friends, Remainers, Conservatives: I come not to praise *nuance*, but to sadly bury it in an unmarked grave.

The period covered in this book charts the continuing journey of a world not long escaped from the vicious Cold War polarity of East and West with its horrifying existential threats. Rather than that ushering in an era of peace through shared humanity as one might have hoped, human society slid inexorably into a morass of myriad new polarities, where believing what you believe to the exclusion of all other beliefs matters more than trying to see the truths you share.

Mathematically we can express it thusly, if so minded (and Tim is):

Subjectivity > Objectivity

The two threads that form the heart of this book, Brexit and the Trump presidencies, are both prima facie examples of this, though I'm sure you can think of plenty more. They play out endlessly, pointlessly on social media. Conflict has been reduced to a personal level like never before. We all have our own Damocletian swords hovering above us.

For example, the Brexit Referendum presumed to say that an issue as complex as the centuries of relations with our closest geographical neighbours could be reduced to yes, or no. For Trump, there is his way and the wrong way, the fake way, the un-American way: there are his people, and there is everyone else, the enemy. Within or without.

He is not alone in our world, nor is he the first in history to play this game. Let's have a list:

- Hitler
- Stalin
- Joe McCarthy
- Putin
- Jehovah
- Simon Cowell

Judge not lest ye not also be judged, eh, Simon? This is a *joke*. Please don't sue us.

We now seem to live in a world of bipolar absolutes, evidenced by leaders who offer us world views centred on ideas of 'us' and 'them'. Russian/Ukrainian, Alt-right/Antifa, Trans/TERF, black/white. Refugees, that flow of displaced persons that have built the western democracies and modified their cultures in a positive way (anyone else suddenly fancy a Chicken Tikka Masala?) over the last three centuries are now characterised as asylum seekers and illegal migrants, to be stopped, caught, rejected, removed, punished.

How did we get here? Remember Michael Gove's "we've had enough of experts"? Maybe what he really meant was that he – and by extension us – had had enough of the kind of complicated answers to complex questions that experts give. "Yes" is so much easier than "Yes, but…" or "that's not really the right question".

Yes/No; Right/Wrong; Good/Evil; Us/Them. These are the absolutes we seem to be clinging to. It's salutary to look back to the last ten years of the last century, after the Berlin Wall had fallen and those old Cold War polarities had blown away on the winds of a joyous, ecstatic Berlin night. Historian Francis Fukayama proclaimed "The End of History" in print and on every TV chat show that would have him. Western governments celebrated their liberal, democratic values as being the only game in town – and yes, the generations that had grown up and become parents since 1945 breathed a sigh of relief as the spectre of nuclear Armageddon that had hung over their days and stalked their nightmares faded.

When did it change? Martin Amis has argued persuasively that it was the moment the *second* plane struck the South Tower of the World Trade Centre on 11th September 2001. The second, because it was seen live by billions. Video of the first plane wasn't seen until days afterwards, but the second was live, and it made it horrifyingly clear that what we were watching was real, cold, transparent evil.

9/11 sparked a whole new generation of conspiracy theories, the exponentially growing internet gave them the ultimate playground and by 2010 they had become one of the primary methods of political expression. In 2016 Donald Trump's advisors, notably Steve Bannon, knew that there was a great wave of internet-spread anger and anti-establishment paranoia that their candidate could surf all the way to the White House. It's arguable that Trump's election is as significant a turning point as the "second plane", particularly when you consider who he replaced: Barack Obama, the first African-American President, who had won in 2008 on a popular tide with twin aspirations: *Hope* and *Change* (for a UK audience, Obama's third slogan "Yes, we can!" made him sound far too much like Bob the Builder, of course.). How could the US have changed so much so fast? Remember that statistically there *must* have been people who voted for Trump in 2016 (and 2020 and 2024) having voted for Obama in 2008 and 2012. That's some big ol' complexity right there. Trump's victory emboldened the right, horrified the left, delighted America's enemies and baffled its grieving friends.

So in 2025 where does nuance come in? Almost nowhere, it turns out. It takes too long, needs too much thought, too much effort. Complexities are just so exhausting, yeah?

And perhaps that's it: we like certainties, we like absolutes and simple answers. For much of Western history, religion gave us those certainties. Many of us may have lost our faith, but we still seem to have a fundamental human need to have something to have faith *in*. Belief in causes, activism, conspiracy theories and the sense of community they bring can all substitute for religious faith. Feeling like you share a belief with lots and lots of other people is comforting: you're not alone. This is why conspiracy theories like QAnon flourished so dramatically during lockdown, when many people were physically alone, and desperate to feel part of something that offered apparently simple answers to the terrifying complexities of Covid-19.

It's hard overstate the role the internet has played in this over the years since 9/11. It's allowed bad ideas and simplistic answers to propagate, literally at the speed of light, and for people to build communities around those ideas. We've come up with words to describe the phenomenon: Echo chamber. What is a church or a monastery or a temple if not a physical echo chamber, where only one acceptable version of the truth, one dogma, is spoken?

'Ok, so this is all well and good', we hear you cry, 'but what's it doing in a book about satire? Why should I care?'

You should care because satire is a vaccine for terrible ideas and oversimplistic answers. When we're writing, we're actively looking for the inconsistencies in an argument, the things that don't make sense in an answer, or just the things that are plain wrong; and we look for those things *because that's where the comedy is*. We're trying to say "hey, have you seen this bit? It's crazy!".

In other words, we're sugar-coating A-grade nuance with laughter, to make it easier to digest. You're welcome.

Chapter Fifteen

Appalled by Trump? Me too.

2017

(The Imitation Game (panel show); ITV. Breaking the News, BBC Scotland; 2017 continues to baffle.)

"I see we're getting a female Dr Who. I'd be happy to get a Dr Who-stays-in the NHS. Male or female."

Working in Trump's White House is a precarious business, perhaps not surprisingly for a President whose TV catchphrase was "you're fired". First to go, just nine days after Trump's inauguration, is Attorney General Sally Yates after she refuses to implement the President's plan to ban immigration from seven Muslim-majority countries. From that point on there is a revolving door in and out of the West Wing, even if there wasn't going to be one from Iran, Iraq, Yemen, Syria, Libya, Somalia and Sudan.

Meanwhile, there is exciting news from space:

NASA announces the discovery of seven earth-sized planets in the Trappist-1 system, 59 light years from earth. Trump says he'll ban immigration from them, too. Inhabitants in the Trappist system were said to be "maintaining a dignified silence."

Geography really isn't one of Donald's strengths (a short companion volume listing his strengths is soon to be available in business card form) as he demonstrates when he says he is considering "buying Greenland" for its strategic importance. Greenland and Denmark (of which Greenland is a part) react with simultaneous outrage and amusement, the Danish Prime Minister Mette Fredriksen saying that it is "absurd" and that "Greenland is not for sale". Trump calls this response "nasty" – an epithet he reserves almost entirely for women he doesn't like, and responds as any spoilt toddler President would by cancelling a planned State Visit to Denmark. The communal sigh of relief issued by the Danish people causes disruption to northern European weather patterns for a month.

He won't let go of the idea. Indeed, hanging on tenaciously to terrible ideas is a Trump speciality and after his Election victory in 2024 (another spoiler alert) he reiterated his desire to buy Greenland and muttered darkly about sending American Troops there to seize it. A tactic straight from the Putin playbook in other words, but one which would produce a very particular dilemma: as both Denmark and the US are members of NATO, any military action against Greenland would require, under the binding terms of the NATO Charter, all members to immediately respond in force. So the US would have to send troops to kick itself out of Greenland, and if that isn't Trumpism in a nuttyshell, we don't know what is.

Back in those you-ain't-seen-nothin'-yet days of his first term in office, Trumpishly bad behaviour is dominating world headlines as the "Me Too" movement progresses from a hashtag to a global phenomenon in a matter of months. Triggered by the welter of sexual assault accusations against Hollywood mogul Harvey

Weinstein, women and men who've been the victims of abuse by the rich and famous feel empowered to bring that abuse to light. It is very much one of those shocked-but-not-surprised events: the casting couch had been a seedy part of Hollywood's mythologising for as long as Hollywood had existed.

Sexual harassers are dropping like their flies.

Kevin Spacey is one of the biggest names to fall far and fast. Appropriately enough, he's playing an amoral President in Netflix's reboot of British political thriller **House of Cards**:

I see House of Cards has been cancelled* after the shocking revelations about Kevin Spacey. Given the accusations already made against Trump this means that Netflix effectively has a better moral compass than Congress. '

(*in fact they just shot the final season without him. Because, you know, money.)

The thing about Trump's accusers isn't simply the sheer number of them, but the callousness with which he dismisses them as liars and condemns any investigations of him as 'witch hunts'. He denies one alleged rape on the grounds that the alleged victim "isn't his type". It beggars belief, but then he does. It's his one consistency, that if there is a dumb, crass, bullying way to do something he'll find it and fully exploit it, whether it's against political opponents, employees or even foreign heads of state.

Following Russia's annexation of the Crimea, which was (and remains) legally part of Ukraine, it doesn't take a genius to see that Putin's territorial ambitions won't stop there, any more than The

Third Reich was going to stop with the Sudetenland. (Quite something, isn't it, when the leaders of both Russia and the US are regularly compared to Hitler?). It is clear that Ukraine will need Western support in the form of arms, materiel and money. Trump speaks to Ukrainian President Vlodymyr Zelenskyy on the phone in 2019, ostensibly to agree the next tranche of American aid. Instead, Trump tries to steer the conversation towards the alleged business dealings of Hunter Biden, the troubled son of Joe and Jill Biden, with the immortal words "I would like you to do us a favour", clearly tying this "favour" to the military aid. There are literally dozens of people listening and recording every word and Trump must have known this. The transcript of the call becomes the central piece of evidence in Trumps first (!) Impeachment Trial. Yet, in his reality-denying way, he continually refers to it as "a perfect phone call".

Is he so tied up in his own lies that he believes them to be true? Or does he know all along that he's lying? Is he a delusional narcissist or a just a psychopath? Hell, Donald would probably say he can do both "better than anyone's ever seen!"

As humans, we are fundamentally social animals, hard-wired to see the good in people. In this respect, as in others, Trump is a complete outlier. Try and think of one good character trait that he demonstrates, or which you even heard of him demonstrating?

The movie opens. Tumbleweed blows gently across an arid landscape. The music of Ennio Morricone can faintly be heard on the hot desert wind. A distant bird mournfully cries. Nothing really happens for three hours. Slow fade to black. Oscars are won by the bucketload.

He doesn't even like dogs, for God's sake. To a British audience this is an instant red flag, a sure sign of outré caddishness. It's telling that Trump's campaign machine has regularly used the Bidens' dogs occasionally bad behaviour as a stick to beat the President: "There's no such thing as a bad dog, just bad owners". One could say the same thing about children and fathers, eh *Donny*?

Humpty Trumpty sat on his wall

Humpty Trumpty had a great fall

All Putin's hackers and all the white men

Couldn't get Trumpty elected again*

*2024 note: feckety-feck feck.

Trump's voters, his base, his "people" either don't care what he does, are so amorally, sociopathically, psychotically screwed themselves that they actually **like** what he does, or have simply drunk the Trump Kool-Aid and are convinced that Trump and only Trump tells the truth. It's his biggest and most fundamental lie: that he isn't a liar. Secondly, it shows his belief that he is legally untouchable. He is the most sued person in America and has won enough of those cases – or had them dismissed by friendly judges - to make him think he will always win. Maths is one of his many, many blind spots.

It was clear in 2016 that he regarded the Presidency as the ultimate *Get Out Of Jail Free* card, and in 2024 it seemed to be most of the reason he was running. When his numerous indictments are being discussed on the US news channels it's standard practice to distinguish between the federal crimes he could pardon himself of as President and the State-level ones he can't. Just read that again. It is insane – as is the fact that there are also regular conversations about whether he could run whilst in prison, and how the Secret Service would protect him if he was incarcerated. We know now that his re-election is indeed the ultimate stay-out-of-jail card, precisely as he'd hoped. While he could be prosecuted when (if) he leaves office in 2029, by then Meta will probably run the Department of InstaJustice and the Attorney General will be the re-animated corpse of Al Capone. Or Rudy Guliani, which is more or less the same thing.

The media seemingly don't know how to handle someone who doesn't just not play by the rules, but seems to be playing a completely different game, one to which they aren't invited. A new approach is needed, one to equip even the youngest in society to be politically literate:

To prepare the under 5's for a life political turmoil, Cheebies are bringing back the the TellyTrumpies:

Putin: TankyWanky

Boris: Dipstick

Farage: LaLa not listening

Trump: PO-tus

Crazy, you see? It's all fake news, of course. Witch-hunt. Etc. Et al. Ad bloody nauseam.

(Tim, that's enough bad Latin, you classically educated numpty. Mary x)

Chapter Sixteen

Education, education, education. Sounds familiar.

2018

(The News Quiz; Tour with Jan Ravens; various media appearances.)

"Education: the systematic learning and application of knowledge. Adult education: wanting to remember something. Anything. Please."

Education is a passion for both of us. Mary's worked in primary schools with Special Needs children and is a qualified TEFL teacher. Tim's the child of two English teachers and has worked in Higher Education as a librarian for over twenty years. Education is traditionally a political football with governments keen to set their ideological brand on a state education system that would prefer to be left the hell alone to just get on with it most of the time.

In January 2018, Theresa May delivers a speech on the future of Higher Education. Tim watches it, throws things at the TV for a bit then writes this, occasionally even pausing for breath.

So, Theresa May finally delivered her much-leaked speech on the reform of University funding, and it's the soggiest of damp squibs, an "independent" enquiry that will have any kind of wholesale change ruled out of its possible conclusions.

The best we'll get is a yet another limp burst of tinkering round the edges, and if the speech is anything to go by, an attempt to blame Universities for not offering "consumer choice" i.e. a range of cheaper options than £9250 a year and not delivering "value for money". This is a profoundly empty concept when we're talking about something so vital to the future of our country, particularly as we venture into a post-Brexit wasteland under Mrs May's excuse for leadership.

This fails on so many grounds, not least that it will be decided and voted on by a generation who went to university for free. This is fundamentally immoral. I'm part of that generation and believe me, the way things are now makes me almost ashamed of how lucky we were.

It fails to recognise the fundamental fact that higher education is a common good. To fund it like this is to make it a luxury, funded by debt. We don't treat schools like this, or defence, or health. Yet.

If the government thinks fewer people should go to university, they should have the guts to say so, and let's have that debate, honestly and openly. Tuition fees will remain, as they have always been, an attempt to shrink the sector by stealth. We're having this "review" because that has not worked and it's costing the government more than funding higher education out of general taxation would. So, yeah, well done this seemingly endless and hopeless Tory government. You couldn't organise a tutored wine tasting in your favourite Tuscan wine bar, you utter bastards.

So: morally, politically, economically, it is simply wrong and it will remain so until a proper, root and branch review of how we as a country fund our higher education happens. In other words, up yours, Mrs May. Is there anything you aren't going to completely ruin?

Very probably the views of my employer but they're not going to say it out loud.

As 2018 progresses, the May premiership becomes ever more surreal. The Tory press office seem to be trying to humanise her by arranging for her to be interviewed on popular TV chat shows. Appearing on The One Show with her husband Philip, while talking about how they divided the household tasks between them, she comments that taking out the bins is "a boy job":

I wonder if Theresa May is starting to think that implementing Brexit is a 'boy job'?

As if this isn't odd enough, on ITV's Tonight programme, Julie Etchingham asks the Prime Minister what the "naughtiest thing she'd ever done" was. May responds by telling a strange story about 'running through a wheatfield as a child'. This mystifies most people, annoys farmers who point out that if she doesn't get the deal done quickly, they won't be able to afford to grow fields of wheat, and it really, really pisses coeliacs off.

All this talk of childhood high-jinks moves us to reimagine some classic party games to reflect the turbulent times we're living in:

Musical Chairs:

Start with twenty-eight chairs, each occupied by an EU Member State. The music starts and the UK gets up and walks round the room ranting about sausages and bent bananas. Their chair is removed. The music stops and the game ends. The winners are the twenty-seven players who still have a chair. The UK loses. About £140bn.

Pass the Parcel

The game is played by the current and all previous Brexit Secretaries. A large, shiny parcel is passed around with each player tearing off a layer of wrapping to reveal a New Deal That Really Will Work (This Time). The game ends when the last layer of paper is removed and the parcel is revealed to contain sod all. Everybody loses.

Blind Woman's Buff

Played by Theresa May, on her own in a small, dark room with a blindfold on. Her task is to construct a Brexit deal that everyone in her party will like, and then sell it to the electorate*. The game ends when she either resigns or has a nervous breakdown.

Variant: Theresa is blindfolded and placed in the room as above but is told she's actually in a wheat field. She runs straight into a wall and the game ends.

*aka the thirteenth task of Hercules. Which were all boy jobs.

Boris Says

A variant of Simon Says where players have to ignore everything that Boris Says. This game is popular in the USA, where it's known as "Trump Says".

Treasure Hunt

All players have to continually reassure Jeremy Hunt that they really, really love him rather than telling him what they actually think: that he's a useless Tory twit.

There's a creeping feeling, particularly within her own party (which has plenty of creeps) that she can't get the job done. It feels like certain cabinet ministers, whose name shall remain Boris, are actively briefing against the Prime Minister. The Tories are almost as good at stabby acts of treachery as they are at conjuring unlikely election victories. They haven't finished on either score.

Theresa is just like Michael Caine at the end of the Italian Job. Except that she doesn't have a great idea, the lads have all jumped off already and the bus is definitely going over the cliff.

I can't seem to sleep at the moment. I think I've got Brexsomnia.

Not for the first time in British political history, the early part of the year is dominated by "the Irish question", in this case as it applies to Brexit. For once, in Westminster, it isn't greeted with cries of "who bloody cares?" or similar self-obsessed British bulldogshit.

The issue is that after Brexit, the border between Northern Ireland and the Irish Republic will become a land border between the UK and the EU. Movement across the border is currently free and open, a key part of the Good Friday agreement that brought an end to thirty years of terrorism in the North, and there is a long and noble tradition of smuggling anything cheaper on one side of the border to the other. A "hard" border with customs checks and security will fulfil the likely needs of Brexit, but also potentially kill the Good Friday Agreement, with God knows what awful consequences.

And of course, the fact that the May government is propped up by the Taliban-in-bowler-hats of the DUP adds yet another layer of horror to Theresa's no doubt regular nightmares.

With 2024 hindsight, we actually feel a *little* bit sorry for Theresa. She really was screwed from day one. Cameron handed her an enormous bucket of manure which almost half her party were loudly convinced contained twenty-four carat gold studded with diamonds. She supported Remain but felt obliged by the referendum result to see Brexit through, and could only have overturned the vote by igniting a bloody civil war in her party, We're quite sure she felt utterly trapped at times.

Back to 2018. The meetings held at Chequers to thrash out a deal once and for all probably also figure prominently in the PM's fever dreams. Of course, they keep their cards close to their chest in public over what the deal might look like. True to form, when there's a vacuum to be filled with a bit of satire, we aren't going to pass up the opportunity.

Secret Agenda for Chequers meeting:

Options for discussion

- *No deal. Noel Edmonds becomes Brexit Secretary.*

- *Single market and customs union, but the words "Odimus modo gallico* to be added to the Union Jack. *'we hate the french'*
- *Norway*
- *Norway plus (i.e. Sweden)*
- *Admit it was all a dream.*
- *Admit it was the equivalent of drunk-buying £200 concert tickets at 3am. (aka Leavers' Regret)*
- *DUP and ERG to go on one-way fact-finding mission to Outer Mongolia.*
- *All arable land in the south east to become wheat fields for Prime Minister's personal use.*
- *Send out for Dominos after three hour discussion over whether that counts as Italian food or not.*

On the twelfth of July, the government publish the 'Chequers Plan' which has been agreed following lengthy talks at the Prime Minister's country seat, chosen presumably because of its proximity to wheat fields. The date is also interesting as May's DUP allies are otherwise occupied that day, marching and generally pissing of people who'd prefer a quiet life where everyone just gets on with each other.

The plan also has some significant opponents: both David Davies and Boris Johnson resign from the cabinet over it. As they are the Brexit Secretary and the Foreign secretary, this is such a huge deal it could be Black Friday, which it isn't. Safe to say, it's a blow from which May's government can never really recover and it's the beginning of a running battle over the shape of Brexit between and within the major parties and with the great institutions of state. Both the House of Lords and the Supreme Court, whose founding had been one of the final acts of Gordon Brown's government, play significant roles in the months to come. That Brown government is now almost eight years dead and Labour in power is becoming a distant memory, as fleeting a thing as opinions in the mind of Boris Johnson. And his love affairs.

Indeed, it almost feels like we've gone back to the Thatcher-dominated years of the 1980s when, surprise surprise, the Tories were hopelessly split over Europe.

Terry Wogan: *Hello, good evening and welcome to this special Conservative Edition of Blankety Blank! All blankety-blank cheques but no cash. Welcome to our panel: Michael Howard, Boris Johnson, Willian Hague and Jacob Rees-Mogg!*

The first question goes to Michael. The solution to conflict in Europe is 'blank'?'

Michael Howard: *'Clearly, nobody wants conflict. All that blood and death and horror and so on.'*

Wogan: *'I might have known you wouldn't actually answer the question! The answer on the card is Collective Security Within the EU, Michael. You need help.*

Now it's your turn, Boris. The EU gave 'blank' to Britain in 2017'?

Boris: *'Is it a load of unnecessary regulations? Yes, definitely!'*

Wogan: *'No, I'm sorry, the answer is seven billion euros, Boris. You never were good with figures, unless they're written on the side of a bus, or in a corset.*

Now, young Master William, here's yours. David Cameron was 'blank' in 2016.'

Hague: *'I know David quite well, I was his foreign secretary, after all. I think the answer is 'an overly optimistic twat!'*

Wogan: *'Spot on! One very British and masculine point to you.*

Lastly, over to Jacob. Jacob Rees-Mogg is a 'blank'.

Rees-Mogg: *'Clearly, I am first and foremost a Conservative, so that ought to be the answer.'*

Wogan: *'Well, Jacob, you're close. It does start with a 'c' but this is a family show. So, after all that nonsense, William Hague is the winner and the rest of the country are the losers.'*

This, by the way, is an excellent example of where the quality of Rory's impressions drive and energise the writing process: all five voices used in this skit are amongst his very best and lift material beyond our expectations. It's a writer's dream.

Further to that, and using another one of Rory's best and most beloved impressions, the opportunity to have Alan Bennett share his feelings on Brexit is too good to miss:

'Do you want to hear what I think about Brexit? Of course you don't. Nobody gives two hoots about what I've got to say. I was saying that to my cleaner the other day, she's Romanian. Not Remainian, sadly, although she'd like to.

She's leaving me next March of course. The 'Send them all Home Office' will see to that. I shall miss her dreadfully, she buffs all my bits up beautifully.

I like Jeremy Corbyn, what with his obsession with jam and cycling and inability to do anything constructive, he's very much like a character in one of my exciting plays.

You don't know who to believe, do you? I said to Mother, that Lord Adonis, dear me, there's a name to live up to if ever I heard one, well he gives me the shivers all those mean things he says about the BBC. Where would I be without the BBC? Probably here, in my armchair, actually, but not so bafflingly famous. I mean, can you see me on ITV, sandwiched between Keith Lemon and Ant and Dec? Would Netflix commission a fifteen part oral history of dull biscuits from me? I think not.

So, Brexit, people were all excited about it at first but after a while it's got all difficult and depressing. Bit like me, really.

Nailed it there, Alan. Opinions about Brexit are like toilets, everyone has one and quite a few of them are full of shit.

Speaking of Boris Johnson, it's increasingly clear that he's aiming firmly for Number Ten, positioning himself as the champion of yes, you guessed it, the Eurosceptic/nutter/bastard wing of the party. They take to calling themselves the 'European Research Group" which is a bit like Dracula listing himself as a "Sanguinary Consultant" on LinkedIn.

(Note to self: pitch idea of Vampire who selects his victims via LinkedIn to Netflix. Working title: The Social Neckwork)

The ERG rival the DUP in the most-rabid-three-letter political-grouping stakes. If they could build a wall in the middle of the

Channel they'd regard it as a logical extension of Brexit. Jacob Rees-Mogg, a bizarre gothic character from an unpublished Dickens horror novella, is one of their leading shites. Sorry, *lights*. But on the other hand….

The ERG begin to fantasise about what becomes known as a "No Deal" Brexit, the (to everyone else) horrific prospect that the UK will leave the EU some time in 2020 and strike out alone in the world, without trading partners, backing or anything very much. Or, if you're Jacob-Rees Mogg, 'bestriding the world as a trading colossus as once the Empire did'. In fact, rather than being the Empire on which the sun never set, it seems likely that a no-deal Brexit will plunge Blighty into something akin to perpetual darkness.

Jacob Rees Mogg explains the current situation: "Everybody wants an election, except that nobody wants one unless there's a deal or a deal on no deal. If there's a deal on a deal or a deal on a deal on no deal, then everyone will want an election but they're all scared of losing it for supporting the wrong deal (or no deal). This is a bum deal, and no-one wants that. I hope that makes things clear"

There's someone else who seems to have similarly dark visions of the UK's future, and indeed present: Vladimir Putin. In March 2018, Russian exile and man not on Putin's Christmas card list, Sergei Skripal and his daughter Yulia are the victims of an almost successful assassination attempt in their adopted home town of Salisbury. This is pretty shocking in itself, but the method used makes it seem like something truly appalling: a nerve toxin known as Novichok, developed by the Soviet Union at the height of the

Cold War, and hidden in a perfume bottle. The Skripals survive, barely, as does a member of the police investigating team.

The government reaction is understandably furious, with Theresa May vowing revenge; 143 Russian Diplomats will be expelled by the end of the month. Of course, Rory is on tour so we need to write jokes about it, but we aren't the only ones: later in the year, the two Russians accused of the dastardly deed by the UK claim in a staged Russian TV interview that they had only been in Salisbury "to visit the Cathedral and buy health products". I mean, LOL, or what?

Theresa May's probably jealous of Putin's Russia being effectively a one-party state. She hasn't even got a one-party party.

You've got to feel sorry for all those high-class perfume companies pumping huge sums of money into advertising campaigns. I don't know about you but I'll never look at a perfume bottle in quite the same way. 'Happy birthday, darling. Bought you a bottle of your favourite nerve agent at the airport.'

Theresa's capacity for revenge on the international stage has been weakened now that she can't send Boris on a visit.

And while we're on the subject, 'Boris' is a pretty Russian-sounding name. Is he a mole? Would explain a LOT.

As the year winds to close, Brexit negotiations continue to run on and on and on, becoming ever more complex and frankly dull. Perhaps this is the plan – get to the point where we'll happily replace being sick of elections with being sick of talking about Brexit? Perhaps, who knows, we might simply vote for anyone, literally *anyone* who promises to "Get Brexit Done".

Whoops, spoilers! Sorry.

Chapter Seventeen

Mostly Not Dead White Men.

2012 – present day.

"I'm so glad we've got another Elon Musk scandal, please can we call this one 'Elongate'? It'll go on, and on, and on…"

"It is easier for a camel to pass through the eye of a needle than it is for a rich man to make a blues record" (Hugh Laurie)

It is, at least in part, the role of satire to speak truth to power, and very often that means political power, and the Governments, Presidents and Prime Ministers who wield it. However, the twenty-first century to date has thrown up a new kind of power in the hands of a generation of billionaires enriched by a welter of new technologies and in particular those associated with the internet. They're overwhelmingly white, male and American. Bill Gates set the pattern of progressing from garage tinkerer to fabulously wealthy CEO, with Steve Jobs doing the same only with better clothes and highly designed, highly priced products. Ok, *Steve*, yes, I've got an iphone and an ipad, Mary's got the phone and the watch, but we're writing this on a Windows PC so yeah, feck you. And you're dead, so we win.

The new generation of billionaires took the world that Gates, Jobs, Tim Berners-Lee and others had built and made money out of it. LOTS of money: most of all Jeff Bezos at Amazon; Nick Clegg's former employer Mark Zuckerberg at Facebook/Meta; and token non-American, Elon Musk. Musk is particularly interesting as he differs from Bezos et al in more ways than nationality. Whereas most of these nouveau super-riche make a very public point of their philanthropy, occasionally verging on virtue-signalling excess (surely not), it's pretty clear that Musk is primarily interested in enriching himself and using his endless pot of gold to gain unwarranted influence. There's a reason he's got both a aerospace company (SpaceX) and owns Twitter/X: he's a space cadet who doesn't know when to shut the hell up. There are numerous occasions when the latter has got him in trouble, like when he concluded the man who masterminded the rescue of a group of Thai schoolchildren from a flooded cave, must be a paedophile – and then said so on Twitter. By the same (il)logic he must think that Santa is a nonce of truly global proportions. It's also notable that one of his first acts as Twitter CEO was to restore Donald Trump's account, which had been closed down, not before time, after he had, you know, tried to mount a coup d'etat on January 6th 2021. It wasn't clear whether Musk did this because he either didn't care or he *really* didn't care. Creep.

This was also a good indication of the rapid rightward drift of Musk's politics, and an increasing fondness for conspiracy theories, and any craziness that crossed his timeline. Following Trump's re-election in 2024, Musk took his previous vocal support for DJT into what amounted to full blown stalking. He started turning up at all kinds of Trumpworld events and apparently moved in to Mar-a-Lego. When the time came for Trump to assemble his cabinet, Elon was given joint control of a newly formed Department of Government Efficiency. The fact that the resulting acronym – DOGE – is the name of Elon's favourite cryptocurrency shows that his ego is rapidly getting too big for the planet. Musk's co-chair at DOGE is announced as being Vikram Ramaswamy, a man once described by Nigel Farage as "the future of American Conservatism". If that doesn't scare you it's possible that you are in fact dead. Thanks for buying the book before you shuffled off this mortal coil first, though. Interestingly, Ramaswamy became the first of many, many people to be sacked by DOGE.

Like Trump, Musk's fanclub is that same internet do-your-own-research-sheeple conspiracy crowd. They don't like most of the oligarchs; Bill Gates in particular has been the negative focus of the nutters (let's be honest) who, amongst other things, have accused him of backing Covid vaccination programmes so he could inject everyone with nano-scale microchips and thereby, I don't know what, take over the world or something? This was clearly nonsense, not least as it was clearly well beyond Microsoft's technical ability, as anyone who's tried to connect a Windows PC to a printer, work on a shared document or use your pc for more than ten minutes without Windows wanting to do a fecking update in really, really needy way can testify. Bezos also apparently has unspecified nefarious goals, as if selling lots of things that people want at good prices and delivering them quickly (most of the Prime) wasn't dastardly enough. The fiend.

So maybe Musk was saying to the conspiracy theorists: 'look guys, I'm one of you. Nothing to see here. Trump likes me! Look, tinfoil hat!' and thereby exempting himself from their fantasies. To be honest, we're hating ourselves for creating the idea of fantasies featuring Elon Musk. Eww.

Elon's basically annexing Bond villain territory like Putin took the Crimea. He even wants to build a base on Mars, which he's said he hopes will have a "fun, outdoorsy atmosphere". Fine, provided you like your *outdoorsing* to be in fifty below zero with no atmosphere to speak of. A nightclub in Murmansk, basically.

If you're reading a tattered and scorched copy of this book in some post-apocalyptic hovel because it turns out our Elon was right to be really, really worried about AI, then please disregard the last few paragraphs. He's a prophet, blessed be his name, his money and his heavenly sportscar. Amen.

Of course there have always been rich people (again, mostly male, mostly white) and no doubt some of them haven't been very nice. Are the current crop any different? They're certainly very rich: it's very hard to picture a billion anything but is there a way to get a sense of it? Try this: if we took the net worth of the ten richest individuals in the world divided that wealth equally between the global population, every single human alive would get around 200 dollars. 8 billion people, $200 each.

And what would we do with it? Buy something from bloody Amazon, on an iphone, while watching the latest SpaceX launch, probably. Or you could all buy a dozen copies of our book!

And maybe that's the difference with these modern moguls: it's obviously, achingly, clearly true that *we made them*. We bought the iWhatevers, snatched up the Lightning Deal, tweeted photos of our breakfast, stalked our exes on Facebook and our children on Instagram, clicked those sponsored links in Google searches and preferred PayPal over cash – and we made them all very, very rich by doing it. So every time you watch another SpaceX rocket spazz itself all over southern Florida, you can feel just a tiny, teeny, little bit of pride and think: *we did that*.

You'll note that we've only mentioned Trump a few times in this chapter and there's a reason for that: he isn't rich. Not at least in the way that Bezos et al are. However, he is very good at pretending he's rich and getting people to believe that he is and treat him accordingly. And of course when we say "people" what we actually mean is "banks". He's a one-man bubble, a pension bond infected with toxic subprime loans made flesh. Yet he gets away with it again and again because the banking shitterati know that he's one of them, part of the collective amoral mammon-worshipping ego of Wall Street. Even when he was found guilty of 34 separate charges relating to various breaches of financial law -including using campaign funds to buy the silence of porn star and fleeting Trump paramour Stormy Daniels there was some evidence it had made him even more popular with his MAGA base. FFS.

In general, for all of these nauseatingly rich men it doesn't really matter what they have or haven't done wrong because the only crime that really matters in the capitalist world is being poor, and for billions, it carries a life sentence.

Nipping forwards to January 2025, the invited audience at Herr Trump's second inauguration/Putsch was a who's-who of Transnational Oligarchy: Musk, Zuckerberg, Bezos and Google CEO Sindar Pichai looking like nothing more or less than the Four Yes-Men of the Trumpocalypse.

Chapter Eighteen

Deal or No Deal?

2019

"Who's going to be next to take the Brexit minister's job? It's become the political equivalent of the defence against the dark arts job at Hogwarts, which is quite appropriate, really"

"So, if we revoke Article 50, do we just move on to Article 51? I've looked it up and it enshrines in EU law the right to imprison Jacob Rees-Mogg indefinitely for the crime of being himself."

In the early part of 2019, Rory is on tour again, and we have the chance to go and see him perform in Cambridge. Tim (like so many Durham graduates, a proud Oxbridge reject) is in the odd position of making himself the butt of a joke:

I have a friend in the audience tonight. Lives in Durham, went to Durham University, so it's nice that he's finally got into Cambridge.

The tour also gives Rory the opportunity to take the temperature of the audiences on the chronically flatulent elephant in the room that is Brexit:

Who's for May's deal? Who's for No deal? Who's for Jeremy's pie in the sky deal, whatever it is? Well, I don't think there's a majority for any of those, so what we'll do is ask you exactly the same question in the second half. I'm sure we'll get a completely different result.

It's like the population has broken down into a number of groups based on their attitude to our impending messy divorce from Europe: Here's a summary of our findings, with examples:

- Don't care. (Sociopaths)
- Don't know, don't care. (Sociopaths in a Coma since 2010)
- Even if I did know, I wouldn't care. (Psychopaths)
- Know but don't care. (Some people, unfortunately.)
- Know, care, wish it would go away (Most people)
- Know, care, want it to happen, then go away. (Most of the rest of the people)
- BREXIIIIIIITTTTTTT! Yeah, baby! (Nigel Farage)
- Hate the French (the ERG)
- Hate everybody who isn't exactly like me. (Jacob Rees Mogg, the unthinking man's Goebbels.)

(Note: Boris Johnson is an example of all the groups, depending on who he's talking to.)

Jeremy Hunt, everyone's favourite cockney rhyming slang, warns us all that Britain "could end up with a No-Deal Brexit by mistake". *By mistake*, Jeremy? Yes, Jezza, *mate*, it's all a mistake. A mistake to hold the referendum in the first place, a mistake not to require a two-thirds majority for change, a mistake to say it was an advisory referendum when it was nothing of the kind. It was a mistake to elect a barely sane crypto-communist arch-eurosceptic as Labour leader when almost anyone else would have won the 2017 election, a mistake to assume that a 52/48 result would be anything other than hopelessly divisive, a mistake to trigger Article 50 like it was going past its use-by date. It was all a massive fecking mistake and somewhere in your frigid Tory heart, you know it. Boris cheerleading for it all wasn't enough of a clue for you?

Speaking of Bojo, he's edging ever closer to the pinnacle of power he so clearly craves: not content with having wriiten a biography of Churchill, he now wants to cosplay him too. Theresa May resigns in March 2019, following the lukewarm (freezing, actually) reception to her Brexit proposal, although she's probably just sick to death of absolutely everyone and everything by this point, and who can blame her?

So, while Theresa dreams of ERG-free wheatfields to run through, yet another Tory Leadership contest gets under way. A positive rogues' gallery of candidates soon present themselves for consideration: Johnson, Michael Gove, Amber Rudd, Jacob Rees-Mogg (the proverbial bad penny*), and Jeremy Hunt, victim of the funniest TV bloopers ever, when the BBC presenter Justin Webb calls him "Jeremy C*nt" live on air. And people say the BBC doesn't tell the truth…

Ed's note: No! Penny Mordaunt didn't stand for leader until 2022.

Oh, and we've forgotten about Phillip Hammond. Just like everyone else does. And always has. Don't even bother Googling him. It isn't worth it.

Tory MP Rory Stewart has also announced his candidacy. Well liked across party lines, with ample real-world experience as a diplomat (in such cushy locations as Afghanistan and Iraq) and politically fluent, he's a candidate who could perhaps unite the party and move it forward into a brighter future. He therefore has absolutely no chance of winning the support of the foul-smelling bag of crazy, feral, rabid tomcats that is the 2019 edition of Tory UK. He's duly one of the first to be voted out and goes on to leave parliament at the following general election, thereby demonstrating in various ways what a thoroughly decent human being he is and exactly the kind of person who should be in politics. But isn't. Sigh.

(Mary's note: Tim is led quietly away at this point, given a cup of tea and the latest Rory Stewart/Alaistair Campbell "The Rest is Politics" podcasts to listen to on a loop. He'll back shortly.)

(Ahem. It was two cups of tea, four podcast episodes and several chocolate biscuits but I'm ok now.)

Soon enough, or perhaps not before time, the field is whittled down to two candidates: someone who makes people think of the word "c*nt" every time they think of him, and Jeremy Hunt. Yes, Boris Johnson is a step nearer to his dream and everyone else's nightmare. A run off vote between the two men ensues, in which rank and file members of the party have a say. Boris wins with a 66% share of the vote and just like that, we have another Prime Minister no-one outside of the jam, Jerusalem and casual racism brigade have voted for.

So. Boris Johnson. Prime Minister. That funny bloke who was Mayor of London and has hair that looks like a repeatedly bombed haystack, as Boris had reportedly been at Oxford, by all accounts. Do you ever hear some outlandish story about Boris that your first reaction to isn't "yeah, that sounds legit."? With anyone else you'd assume it was bollocks. Not with BoJo.

This latest plot twist in Johnson's daytime soap existence takes some getting used to, although perhaps the three years we've had getting used to the idea of President Trump has helped. A little.

At times of trouble like this many of us fall back on the wisdom of the past: we update a few proverbs to reflect the realities of Brexit Britain:

> *A bird in the hand is worth £350m on the bus*
>
> *A poor workman always gets the job as all the Polish ones have gone home.*
>
> *Beggars should not be the Brexit secretary*
>
> *Cast not a vote till May be out.*
>
> *Charity begins at home, but never at the Home Office.*
>
> *Don't shoot the messenger, but don't vote for her either. Then shoot her anyway.*
>
> *Jeremy of all trades unions, master of none.*
>
> *All work and no play makes Jack no longer subject to the Working Time Directive.*
>
> *You can tell more lies with money than...actually just money.*
>
> *A supply chain is only as strong as its frictionless border.*

A house divided against itself can't stand Theresa.

Ignorance is blissfully unaware of the consequences of a no-deal Brexit.

The Troubles shared is a majority halved.

A Home Office decision a day keeps the Polish doctors and nurses away.

A friend to everyone definitely isn't an MP

April showers of shite bring forth May's resignation.

Do not carry coals to Newcastle without a mindbending amount of paperwork.

Early to bed and early to rise makes a presenter of the Today Programme.

Eat, drink and be merry, for tomorrow everything's going to cost more.

Fools rush out where angels fear to tread.

Etc, etc…

Does it help? We feel better, but not for long because it's now the case that Brexit's cheerleader in chief is in 10 Downing Street and any hope of reversing the "decision" to leave begins to fade faster than a greased-up rat up a drainpipe. Which is also a convenient metaphor for Johnson's rise to power.

To his credit (really, fairs fair), Johnson always seems much less comfortable with his lack of a clear mandate and reliance on the nutters in the DUP than Theresa May had (or as various Tory PMs would have in the years ahead). It is still something of a surprise when in November 2019, he announces, with more snap than a dodgy busload of crackers. that we are all getting a General Election for Christmas on December 12th.

A simple and dignified message is relayed to the world via a spokes-elf from the North Pole:

"Ho fecking Ho."

Chapter Nineteen

Boing! BJ bounces back.

2019-2020

"People say I should be more respectful towards Boris now he's Prime Minister - that I should respect the office. I will when he does."

"He [Lloyd George] can't see a belt without hitting below it." (Margot Asquith)

Boris Johnson is a man who's perpetually benefitted from being underestimated by – well, just about everyone. They thought he wouldn't be Mayor of London. That he wouldn't get re-elected as Mayor of London. Foreign Secretary? Pah. Prime Minister? Don't make me laugh. BORIS? Yet he did, was, and is all of those while generally being perceived by many as a clownish stereotype of the posh Tory idiot.

Add to this the idea that surely, SURELY, the electorate will do what the people of London and the Tories had failed to do and chuck him out on his ear at the first opportunity? Yet, when all the bluster of a rare winter election fought in suitably blustery winter weather is done, Johnson looks forward to celebrating Christmas in Number Ten with a humongous majority on a 43.6% vote share, the party's largest since the Tory landslide of 1979, and more than any of New Labour's rightly celebrated and sizable victories. Eighty bloody seats, for goodness' sake.

Turnout: 32,014,110 (67.3%, down 1.5%)

	Votes	Vote Share	Seats
Conservative	13,966,451	43.6% (up 1.2%)	365 (up 47)
Labour	10,295,912	32.2% (down 7.8%)	203 (down 59)
SNP	1,242,380	3.9% (up 0.8%)	48 (up 13)
Lib Dem	2,371, 861	7.4% (down 0.5%)	12 (up 4)
Brexit Party	644,257	2% (up 2%)	0 (first election)
Green	865,707	2.7% (up 1.1%)	1 (no change)

We ask the same question so many times in this book - how on earth has it happened? As with the Brexit referendum, many who voted for someone else are seemingly mystified as to how anyone could have voted for Boris, when to them he is so completely unacceptable.

"We were right, how could we have lost?"

This is something that has characterised the way society and politics have changed since the turn of the century – we choose to vote for Party A and everyone we know also votes for Party A (and signals it loudly on social media) so how can Party B (B for Boris) have won? Where this gets problematic is an assumption made by the acolytes of A that people who ticked the B box must be:

- Stupid
- Plebs
- Stupid Plebs
- Old People
- Stupid, plebby old people.

This doesn't help at all, to put it mildly – and hardly anyone puts anything mildly anymore.

And of course the B voters think that Party A's supporters are most likely

- Stupid
- Common
- Snowflakes
- Hoodies
- IRA supporters.

Boris had gone into the campaign with a clear message;

> *"Let's get Brexit done!"*

…and it turns out to be a very seductive message: it resonated for people who have, in large numbers, and crucially, *across traditional party lines*, voted Conservative, many for the first time in their lives. It's millions of little personal dramas being played out with a ballot paper and an annoyingly short pencil. It is…democracy, and the essence of democracy is that sometimes we get the result we don't want and the other guy wins.

And this time, the archetypical Other Guy *does* win. The Tories sweep the "Red Wall", a swathe of seats in the north of England that had been the safest, most secure Labour seats since at least the Norman Conquest. Places where a broken recycling bin with a dead polecat in it could normally have been elected as long as it had a red *Labour* rosette on it. It's the final act of a long, bitter war within Labour between a largely pro-European parliamentary party (except the leader and his increasingly small number of chums) and a grass roots and Trade Union movement which hates the European project viscerally. Many had voted Leave, particularly in Labour's previously safer-than-safe northern heartlands. The shock in Labour circles is deep and palpable, and someone is (finally!) going to have to pay the price for such a dismal performance.

It's clear from election night that that person will be Labour Leader and Gen Z mass karaoke hero Jeremy Corbyn. Under him, Labour have lost two elections against widely unpopular and divisive Tory governments perceived by many as corrupt and self-serving. Corbyn's attempt to rewild the Labour party by pushing it back and back and back to the left has, so far, failed miserably. Too much of the electorate simply don't want to know and probably don't care either.

Perhaps there are even people who'd voted Remain but were so sick of all the endless to-and-fro of negotiations apparently going nowhere that the idea of "Getting Brexit Done" actually seems appealing. Just to not think, talk, hear or even, God forbid, write jokes about it anymore sounds….nice. Nice. Quiet. No shouting.

The other factor that hands Boris the astonishing majority is, , Nigel "Bloody" Farage – just as we all thought we'd heard the last of the unthinking man's blokey twit. UKIP of old is now recast as "the Brexit Party" and early polls show them doing well in the kind of leave-voting constituencies the Tories desperately need to win to get a working majority. Talks in smoke and rash promise-filled rooms no doubt follow and the Brexit Party agree to stand aside in those constituencies where a splitting of the pro-Brexit vote might, horror of horrors, hand the seat to Labour or even (gasp!) the Lib Dems, who (shock) want to *reverse* Brexit, the mad fools. For Farage and his co-conspirators, driving the UK off the European cliff is fine as long as it's them with their brogue-clad feet stamping on the accelerator.

The result of all this is that with Boris in Downing Street, Theresa May can go to backbench solitude and the Corbynistas can go back to being convinced only they are virtuous and right about everything without all that tiresome business of trying to convince the public of the same thing. Depending on your point of view, Jeremy Corbyn is either the Greatest Prime Minister we never had, or someone rightly on target to a quiet retirement and a school patrol man's lollipop plus oversized dayglo overcoat. Don't even try to pretend for a single second that you can't picture that. He'd be a wonderfully benevolent Lollipop Man/Prime minister, once again it's all down to personal opinion.

So this is where we are, as Christmas comes and goes in a rustle of tinsel and 2019 ticks over into 2020 with the usual fireworks-and-prosecco hoopla. Brexit will, for good or ill, finally *happen*. It will all be done and dusted and things can go back to normal, right? 2020 will be better. Has to be better. A new decade and all that. Go us.

Right?

Chapter Twenty

Crying with laughter.

1967 – present day.

Tim on being funny about things that just aren't funny.

Two Ukrainians meet up: One guy asks the other: "So what's going on with the war? What are people saying?".

His friend replies: "What are they saying? They're saying Russia is fighting NATO!".

"Are you serious? How's it going?"

"Well, 70,000 Russian Soldiers are dead, their stockpile of missiles has been almost depleted and much of their equipment has been destroyed!".

"Wow! What about NATO?"

"NATO? NATO hasn't even arrived yet"

(Joke told by Vlodymr Zelenskyy to David Letterman)

The world is full of things that are transparently funny, that it's simple and easy to laugh at. Small children's inappropriate *bon mots*. Dogs. *Gavin and Stacey*. *Frasier*. Ireland beating England at rugby (quite a personal one, that, Tim). Morecombe and Wise. Clowns. John Cleese in *Fawlty Towers*. George Galloway.

It's also full of things that are equally transparently NOT funny. War. Famine. Pestilence, wastes of human life on both personal and genocidal scales. Clowns. Everything John Cleese did after *Fawlty Towers*. And George Galloway.

The next few chapters are, I'm afraid, going to positively reek of the not-funny: COVID, Trump in Power. Boris in Power. War in Ukraine. Should we tell jokes about such things? You bet we should, not least because I can tell you for nothing that there were some amazing, tasteless, brazen, foul and hilarious jokes being told in isolation wards, care homes, the West Wing, Commons bars, police stations, the trenches in the Donblas and bomb shelters in Kyiv. How do I know? Because I was there. Not any of the places just listed, thank God, but Belfast, where I lived from 1967 to 1985, sits unhappily well in that list.

And let me tell you, some of the jokes in Belfast, at my school, on my street, on the buses I used and among my friends were *spectacular*. Beyond simply tasteless they were frequently cruel, graphic, vile and very, very FUNNY. We were literally laughing in the face of death and folly and hatred. Those jokes were inextricably bound to that place and time – because humour is an inoculation against terror, a furious, visceral choir of the damned. I won't repeat any of them here because they belong in and to that place and time, and an individual joke isn't the point, anyway. It's the power of the right joke, at the right time, in the right place. *That's* what matters.

Perhaps one of the greatest examples of comedy born out of transparent horror is the American sitcom M*A*S*H, which ran from 1972 till 1983, following the staff of a Mobile Army Surgical Hospital during the Korean War. The fact that the show debuted in the dying days of the Vietnam War made its satire all the more vital. They rewrote the rule book of what was possible in a sitcom, tore it up, then wrote another even better one. Death stalked the makeshift operating rooms and battered tents of the unit and its theme song was released as a single called "Suicide is painless". It never, never forgot – or allowed you to forget – that war is a stupid, bloodily messy, often pointless business. Yet it is also achingly, hilariously funny. If you've never seen it, treat yourself. You will laugh and you will cry, often at the same time. It's just so real, and that reality is why it is both comic and tragic.

This why I write satire. Why I *have* to write satire. I simply don't have any other healthy way to channel the rage I feel at the murderous fools who blighted my childhood and the childhoods of multiple generations and ended the lives of so many children, fathers, mothers, aunts, uncles, lovers and friends. Who still blight and kill, wherever there are humans to kill and be killed, because the murderous fools – the greedy and stupid - are everywhere, and we just cannot, **must not** let them win. We can't, because then we *all* lose. It's why it's really important that politics works, that we treasure our right to vote and use it wisely, because if we fail to do that, it can let the hateful fools win. It doesn't matter if it's Jacob with inhumane policies, Jimmy with a petrol bomb or Vladimir with a nuclear arsenal, they are schoolyard bullies and we must confront them, defy them, and laugh, laugh, laugh at the bastards. Which they hate because they take themselves so very, *very* bloody seriously.

No, Jacob. No, Jimmy. No, Vlad. Damn the lot of you to hell for a miserable, fiery eternity. The kind you've worked so hard to create on Earth.

I know I sound angry, that's because I still am. A certain amount of the proceeds of this book will pay for my ongoing therapy. That's a necessity because I still have nightmares about burning buses, flinch every time a car backfires or a helicopter flies too low over the house. The largest army helicopter base outside of West Germany was behind the art department at my Belfast school. Think about that, think of it at your school, or god forbid, your child's school. I swear, sometimes, I don't know how my parents slept at night. Maybe they didn't.

When life becomes mere survival, there is nothing more human, no more authentically human response than our ability to laugh, and to make each other laugh. And when implacable, incomprehensible nature threw a terrifying virus at us, when we all had to stay at home, and wear masks and wash our hands for ever? I'm willing to bet that you laughed a lot, saw things on social media that made you howl and for one minute, one second, a fleeting instant, **forget**. Laughed at yourself, your family, your friends and their weird Zoom backgrounds, their scene-stealing pets and children.

You forgot. That's a superpower, right there.

Defy them. Confront them. Mock them. Survive. And *laugh at them like the pitiful godforsaken swine they are..*

Right, let's do COVID.

Chapter Twenty-One

Mask the Family.

2020-2021

"Nearly all men can stand adversity, but if you want to test a man's character, give him power." (Abraham Lincoln)

"We have it totally under control. It's one person coming in from China, and we have it under control. It's going to be just fine." (Donald Trump)

As we write (in 2024/5), the inevitable Public Inquiry into COVID is ongoing in the UK and we, like them, have the benefit of 20/20 hindsight as we look back on the pandemic. However, unlike them, we're not spending vast amounts of both time and public money and can be as smug in an if-we-knew-then-what-we-know-now kind of way if we want to be. So here we jolly well go, me triple-vaccinated hearties. Arrr.

It's in times of crisis that we care most – and it matters most - who our leaders are, and what they do. We celebrate most those who lead us successfully through those times. For the British, this is exemplified by Winston Churchill, and it's perhaps ironic that one of Boris Johnson's projects before he became Prime Minister was to write a biography of Churchill. Who knows how this may have influenced his premiership? Perhaps we should be glad that he didn't become obsessed about Germany being a threat to world peace.

When he takes power, Boris clearly sees his role as being cheerleader-in-chief for Brexit, and a freewheeling ambassador for a new 'Global Britain'. To be fair, he'd probably be quite good at that: even his most visceral and vocal critics concede that he has the gift of the gab – but history has other plans for him, and the rest of us. The cheerleader has to become something between a public school housemaster overfond of moral lecturing and – well, a cheerleader who hasn't made it on to the team this year and hates everyone because of it.

The Americans are, perhaps, even worse off. In Trump, they have someone so self-obsessed, so untroubled by morals and with such a difficult relationship with the truth that half of the population believe every word he says, no matter how bizarre, and the other half don't believe anything he says, even in the unlikely event that it's true. Not really the person to be relied on to deliver vital public health messages at a time of unprecedented crisis. The fact that he has spent several years becoming increasingly paranoid about China's growing world influence make it even worse: he has been referring to climate change as "a Chinese Hoax" and generally using China as a convenient bogeyman to blame for just about anything. Sure enough, within weeks he's referring to Covid as "the China virus", thus making it sound a) fiendish and b) like a horribly dated Jane Fonda movie, i.e. like all Jane Fonda movies.

The idea that there would be a pandemic at some point has been widely discussed, predicted and simulated since the turn of the century, indeed there had already been a positive glut of didn't-quite-make-the-grade infectious diseases, the Gary-Barlow-solo-career kind of pestilence. Things which had failed to kill millions of us include:

- SARS
- MERS
- CJD
- New Variant CJD
- New improved CJD washes your brain whiter than white.
- Swine Flu
- Bird Flu
- One Flu over the Cuckoo's Nest
- Social Influenzas (requiring the wearing of an Elon Mask)

Of course, sugar, alcohol, drugs and cigarettes have killed lots and lots of us but that doesn't seem to count in these sorts of lists as it's probably our own fault for getting addicted to the damn things. In first place, of course, is that ever popular and lethal combination of guns and stupidity, but the only cure for that is brain death, although in some extreme cases, brain death appears to happen long before the death of the rest of the body.

Where, when and how COVID actually started is an ongoing source of debate. Was it a live market in Wuhan? Was it a lab leak from a lab in Wuhan that specialised in coronaviruses? Did it arrive on a meteorite that landed in Wuhan and hit the suspiciously relevant laboratory there? For further details see approximately 28.7% of the entire internet. The fact is that it *has* emerged, is very nasty indeed and is defying all initial attempts to minimise or contain it. A bit like *Love Island* or the mystifyingly long and bafflingly successful TV career of Greg Wallace. (By the way, that line was written in the spring of 2024 and has taken on many new resonances since then. Nostradamus, Mystic Meg *et al* eat your hearts out).

The virus is identified and gene-sequenced by the Chinese remarkably quickly (hmm), and this enables scientists across the world to begin the hunt for a vaccine. However, it turns out that what it *isn't* matters more at first than what it *is*. And what it *isn't* is Influenza. Every planning exercise, every simulation, all the stockpiling of masks, gowns and adult colouring books had assumed that the next Pandemic would be some form of endemic animal flu that had become transmissible between humans. After all, the last one, in 1918-22, the so-called "Spanish Flu" had killed somewhere around 100 million, although we'll never really know exactly how many died. The study that came up with that 100 million figure admitted that they could be out by up to 50 million either way, which basically means we have no idea. The idea that something so world-shakingly enormous could happen and not be recorded in forensic detail shows just how much the world has changed in the last century.

(We don't call it Spanish Flu any more, by the way, because British racists kept trying to emigrate to it. It's now called "You can't drink the water and no one speaks English Influenza". Scientifically it's now known as Influenza Novellum Faragium.)

By a cruel coincidence, it turns out that all the masks that have been stockpiled are designed to stop the large flu virus: the much smaller coronaviruses can sail straight through the (relatively) not-so-tiny holes in the masks. Governments worldwide have warehouses full of paper products of even less use then the Lib Dem "Our plans for power" manifestos. A scramble to source and purchase supplies becomes the focus of entire government departments, and the dark satanic mills of 24-hour TV news with only one story to report, obsess about it.

Before this, PPE had stood, for those who cared, for "Philosophy, Politics and Economics" and it turns out these are actually some quite useful headings to analyse governments' response to the crisis:

The UK

Philosophy: Project Fear II: Chaotic grab bag of strategies. Contact tracing, herd immunity, panic, lockdown.

Politics: Boris, Boris, nearly not Boris, Boris again.

Economics: Rishi Sunak's furlough scheme saves millions of jobs. Probably wise and essential but my God we are paying for it, and our great-grandchildren will still be paying for it sometime next century.

The USA

Philosophy: Blame China, do nothing, despite secretly admitting it's going to be horrendous. Ignore medical advice and suggest things that vary from the simply barking (shining bright light inside the body) to actively lethal (drinking bleach).

Politics: Trump, furiously viewing the pandemic as election interference by Mother Nature. Mother Nature placed in Texan internment camp and separated from her children.

Economics: Too little, too late. Have some fentanyl.

New Zealand:

Philosophy: We're Middle Earth. No Admittance except on Party Business.

Politics: Jacinda Arden, on a journey from being worshipped like Galadriel to being loathed like Sauron.

Economics: Can't make any Lord of the Rings films for 2 years. Economy collapses faster than an England scrum against the All Blacks.

Russia

Philosophy: Deny that they had anything to do with the origins of the virus, whilst secretly acknowledging that releasing a deadly virus is completely the kind of thing they'd do, and then deny. Recall all Russian nationals from Wuhan whilst not blaming China in any way, shape or form. Develop own vaccine and name it *Sputnik* to make everyone notice that it's the first time since 1957 that Russia did anything good first.

Politics: Several Putins continue to be president(s) for life. They all insist on taking their shirts off before being injected with vaccine.

Economics: Oligarchs desperately looking for a way to make even more money out of the pandemic.

(Jeff Bezos says "hold my beer")

Germany:

Philosophy: Immensely relieved that this was an awful, tragic global disaster causing millions of deaths that wasn't even slightly their fault.

Politics: SOMEONE ACTUALLY BLOODY SCIENTIFICALLY LITERATE.

Economics: Economy was already screwed by bailing out the Eurozone anyway, what's another trillion of sovereign debt between friends, jah?

China:

Philosophy: Not telling.

Politics: Not telling.

Economics: What part of "not telling" is it that you don't understand, imperialist lackey? PS please keep buying stuff from us.

France:

Philosophy: Finally get to stop anyone who isn't French entering the country. Rejoicing in the streets would have happened at any other time.

Politics: Macronomics.

Economics: Everyone in the country goes on strike to protest about not having to go to work.

Canada:

Philosophy: Nobody cares.

Politics: Nope.

Economics: Not even a little bit.

Australia:

Philosophy: *see Canada.

Politics: *see Canada.

Economics: *even less than Canada,

The first UK lockdown comes in to effect on March 20th 2020 and for the first time in British history, the entire country throws a collective sickie. There follows a Spring that is utterly remarkable in many, many ways. For a start, the sun shines for weeks on end. It is warm and pleasant. We aren't really able to go out in it, but still. Someone with too much spare time on their hands (which is everyone, to be honest) works out that had a normal English cricket season gone on in April, May and June of 2020 not one single minute, ball or over would have been lost to bad weather. Bear in mind that it is only two years since snow had stopped play at Durham in late April.

Meanwhile, we're all developing a new vocabulary: lockdowns, super-spreader events, R numbers, RNA Vaccines and so on, all brought to us by nightly briefings led by Boris "Prime Minister" Johnson, flanked by various scientists who explained the things Boris can't, i.e. everything of significance, while the whole static three guys behind podiums make it look like Kraftwerk have finally sold out. Of course, many people pay little attention to the briefings, and as a result don't know their R Number from their elbow.

Chief Medical Officer Chris Whitty appears nightly on our televisions, calmly reminding us to stay at home, wear masks and sing 'happy birthday to Covid' while washing our hands. He rapidly becomes an unlikely sex symbol among the middle age mums, who hot flush each time he's on. Although the hot flush could also be the first symptom of Covid.

So what do we all do while this is going on? We bang saucepans, learn how to use Zoom, rediscover our families, boardgames and jigsaws and remember why we'd stopped enjoying them in the first place. We go for tentative walks and try really hard not to look like we're enjoying it, we fall in love with Captain Tom and Andrew Cotter's dogs. Bookshelves have never been so meticulously organised, forgotten attic contents so intently pored over. So many memes – so much of everything overshared on Facebook.

What we do most of all, of course, is this:

WE ORDER STUFF AND HAVE IT DELIVERED.

So much stuff and so many deliveries. Groceries, takeaways, boardgames and jigsaws, facemasks, lateral flow tests, books, kitchen gadgets, novelty face masks, cheap Chinese made disco lights and bubble machines, and so on. And that's just our Amazon purchase history for May 2020. The world is delivered to our socially distanced doorsteps and new mathematics has to be invented to describe how rapidly Jeff Bezos' wealth is increasing.

Where once it had mattered what car you drove in to do your shopping, now the possession of a supermarket delivery slot in the next seven days becomes a source of unrestrained celebration: imagine then, dear reader, how it feels to be classed as "vulnerable" by Sainsburys and gifted a slot. Every. Bloody. Week? Oh yeah, baby.

Tim still hasn't forgiven Waitrose for treating him like, you know, everyone else.

So how do we feel about all of this?

We come to find new love for our homes and deeper appreciation for those we share them with, for our friends and family both near and far.

OR

We realise that we truly loathe our houses, with their unhelpful layout, unpleasant location and lack of outside space and become ever more puzzled why we ever, ever wanted to get married and have children, and as for the weekly family Sunday Night Zoom Charades, well, they and that can just sod off. I hate my life.

(Delete whichever does not apply)

As 2020 ends, it does seem like there's light at the end of the tunnel, and there is a faint chance it isn't a train, but a big old shiny hypodermic syringe.

Chapter Twenty-Two

Ceci n'est pas un conspiracy theory.

(A Brief History of the Ridiculous Tosh People Believe.)

2020-21

"We're jabbin'
(see)
I wanna jab it wid you
We're jabbin', jabbin',
And I hope you like jabbin', too"

(NOT Bob Marley)

"Do your own research, sheeple!"

(Twits on the internet)

Vaccines usually take time to develop. A LONG time. Long, like the gap between Kate Bush albums or Labour election victories. You get the idea. With COVID, that clearly isn't going to be good enough, and with Trump and Boris and their ilk we already have plenty of things that aren't bloody good enough. Across the world, people are dying in ever growing numbers with medics seemingly powerless to do anything except slow the inevitable process of the disease. Italy and then New York become terrifyingly dystopian, fast. Really fast.

A vaccine is needed, fast. Really, really fast.

Over to you, science. Yes, science. The science that distressing numbers of people have spent most of the twenty-first century disregarding, misunderstanding and generally pooh-poohing, whether it's about climate change, evolution, the zillions spent discovering the Higgs Boson or yes, you guessed it, vaccines.

In 1998, some startlingly bad research by a now struck-off Doctor called Andrew Wakefield had suggested a causal link between vaccines and autism, and lots of people had believed it, and were in some cases put through hell believing that that they'd caused their child's autism by getting them vaccinated. We've gone from Goebbels "the bigger the lie, the more people will believe it" to 'the more ridiculous the conspiracy theory, the more of the internet will be devoted to it. Thus, in just a few years we've had the following foist upon us:

The "Mandela Effect"

People claiming to "remember" that Nelson Mandela died at some point before becoming beloved President of South Africa and modeller of rugby jerseys, or that Rice Krispies used to be Rice Crispies, or that New Zealand isn't where we thought it was (no, not Middle Earth).

Yes, I "remember" having my keys at some point, but does that mean that a) they have ceased to exist or b) I know where they are now? It does not. No no no. The Mandela Effect refers to people who don't pay attention to the news, or anything very much, mistaking ignorance for mystery. Idiots.

Qanon

Our theory is that Qanon is possibly the greatest piece of high-concept improvisational comedy ever, and that someone (probably Sacha Baron Cohen or Chris Morris) will emerge from their metaphorical parents' basement at some point and say "gotcha!"

If only this were true. In fact, the Qanon conspiracy theory is a hellish, nightmarish smushing together of some of the following:

- The internet
- Smart phones being used by dumb, paranoid people.
- Everyone having waaaaay too much spare time during the pandemic.
- Donald Trump and his ongoing allergy to the truth.
- Achingly profound levels of stupidity and gullibility.
- Angry white guys.
- With guns.

While it started off riffing on ideas about a global network of child-abducting liberal politicians operating out of the basement of a New York pizzeria, whoever kicked Qanon off was both really clever and terrifyingly irresponsible. What they did was create an all-purpose kit of crazy: whatever your kind of crazy was there was something under the Qanon banner that made you feel it was someone else's kind of crazy too.

This was all very fine and pleasant (perhaps not) but then January 6th happened, the self-proclaimed "Qanon Shaman" became a globally recognisable figure and nothing was fine, and unpleasant didn't even begin to cover it.

2012

The Mayan long count calendar supposedly "ran out" in 2012 and this produced a lot of chatter about the end of the world, supposed hidden planets emerging to destroy earth, and at least one *really* bad movie. As a species we're obsessed with the end of the world and we've been generating theories about it since for ever. It's mortality, of course. It's not the fact that the world is going to end that bothers us, it's the inescapable, universal fact that we *will* end and the world will carry on just fine without us. Sorry.

But what do we know? Tim's just a politics graduate whose idea of a good time is binge-watching videos of John Curtice doing elections analyses on Youtube. Pffft. Meanwhile, Mary knits Dr Who scarves while bingeing on reality television.

Boris is an alien

This is ours. We just refuse to accept that we're the same species as that trumpeting buffoon and if the aliens are all like him, we really have absolutely nothing to worry about.

It's a comforting thought – and maybe *that's* the point of conspiracy theories: that we *want* there to be some big plan in the background that explains everything we don't like about life, because the alternative is that we live in a vast, incomprehensible and uncaring universe in which we simply don't matter one little bit. We are ants poised beneath a giant cosmic boot. It's much more appealing to think that we're part of something that matters. For some of us it's sport, or music, reality TV or religion. An ever more interconnected world has opened up a Pandora's Box of existential cybercomfort. Who are we to say that's not something we should all be entitled to? Until it makes us attack public buildings in an attempt to overthrow an elected government because we wanted the other guy to win and he's as crazy as us.

Back to science, which has, thank God, not taken collective offence at people dismissing the centuries of scientific enterprise because they've "done their own research". In many ways, what happens next is gobsmacking, even to those of us who think it's probably best to let *researchers* do the research. Multiple teams across the world start working on vaccines, rapidly and extraordinarily. The vaccine we will all come to know as "AstraZeneca" is designed on a laptop and created in a lab where they never needed to have a single SARS-COV19 virus. This is science fiction stuff happening in the real world. Ok, not the starships-and-warp drive kind of science fiction but I can wait and the vaccines are a teeny bit more pressing.

Soon we are all rolling up our sleeves and having a minor miracle injected into our veins. No conspiracy, just working together. No theory, just practical science and technology.

Yay us.

Of course, not everyone is so keen to roll up their sleeve. Many people aren't keen on being part of what they see as a very large clinical trial and there is no shortage of celebrity naysayers to prop up popular skepticism. In many ways, the biggest incentive for getting a jab, beyond the health benefits, is all the things you can do once you're vaccinated that are closed to the unvaccinated hold-outs. You can go *out*. You can go *on holiday*. Go back to work in the *office* (it isn't all good) and generally start to have something resembling a normal life again.

Slowly, slowly, life becomes more normal, albeit with fewer grandparents. Never mind, they probably voted Leave.

Covid goes from Pandemic to endemic and we all revert back to having flu, colds, norovirus and other such joys: infectious diseases whose numbers diminished sharply during the pandemic, not least because we were wearing masks and *washing our bloody hands properly*.

Hey ho. Can't have everything.

Chapter Twenty-Three

Party like it's not 2020.

2020-22

"Hear no evil and speak no evil, and you won't get invited to cocktail parties" (Oscar Wilde)

It was reasonably necessary for work purposes" (Boris Johnson on Partygate)

It's worth recalling that the British Prime Minister almost died of Covid, and the US President's brush with the disease stopped him tweeting for almost 12 hours. We never really knew how ill Trump actually was, and those of us old enough were forcibly reminded of the Soviet era leaders stated as "having a cold" when they had actually been dead for three weeks. Ultra-manflu, if you like.

We began this book with a Conservative/Lib Dem coalition government claiming that we were "all in it together" but now, it seems, we actually are. We are all prey to the same virus, the same rules, the same anxieties – and that matters when we aren't able to visit elderly or dying relatives, visit friends or do anything much more than Zoom quiz nights with relatives or friends you are growing to hate the virtual sight of.

Boris managed to bluster his way through most of the controversies that beset his political career – and there were a lot - and mostly have a jolly good time while doing so. It's therefore quite appropriate that his eventual downfall comes about because he was having a jolly good time when no-one else was allowed to. "Partygate", as it becomes known, concerns the fact that various shindigs had gone on in Downing Street during lockdown in 2020 and 2021. We had already seen the downfall of Health Secretary Matt Hancock following leaked CCTV footage showed him kissing someone who wasn't his wife in a Whitehall corridor. He was forced to resign and received the ultimate humiliation of being on *I'm A Celebrity…* where he was dragged over the coals by his campmates in a way that Jeremy Paxman would have been proud of, albeit making it verge on being cringingly unwatchable.

Partying when it isn't appropriate to do so is most likely something that Boris has frequently been guilty of but this is different. In early 2022, the Metropolitan police open an enquiry into no less than twelve gatherings in government and Conservative party offices over the period of lockdown.

> *"On the first day of lockdown*
>
> *My PM gave to me, a party that shouldn't be"*

Video of a fake "news conference" which took place on 22nd December 2020 emerge which show Press Secretary Allegra Stratton joking about a party which took place in Downing Street four days previously. It gives the distinct impression that a party has indeed happened and those present knew it was in breach of lockdown rules. Tim thinks his dad drove a canary yellow *Austin Allegra* in the seventies, by the way.

Once again, we are transparently not *all in it together*: at a time when millions of us are making daily sacrifices of all kinds to keep within the rules. We've just realised that sounds like we're ritually killing goats to appease the clearly angry gods. Or is that just us?

Boris tells Parliament that he is "furious" about the video (I bet he is) and says in response to a question about the alleged party:

"...I am sure that whatever happened, the guidance was followed, and the rules were followed at all times"

Ah, but which rules, Boris? Charades? Mornington Crescent? Twister? Marquis of Queensbury's Drinking games?

Over the following months, more and more reports of clearly illegal gatherings emerge in the media, making Boris' earlier statements look ill-judged at best and downright lies at worst. It seems that, at last, Johnson's Teflon coating is beginning to flake off and his hold on Number 10 is becoming ever more precarious.

Local elections in May loosen his grip on power even more, with the Tories losing almost 500 seats to almost every other main party. How distant the dizzy heights of November 2019's triumphant landslide must seem. Disquiet reigns within the parliamentary party, and Cabinet is becoming not quiet at all. In July of 2022, 62 holders of Cabinet posts resign, forcing Boris's hand. He is done. Done, done, done, DONE, as Beethoven had it. He resigns on 7th July 2022, almost two years since he'd first entered Number 10 as PM, and only 18 months since he'd won that shocking 80 seat majority and gone on to finally push Brexit through. That fact alone will make him a hero in right-wing circles and on one level we know that in writing terms (the write-wing?) we will miss him because he is fun to write about, Rory's impression of him is both uncanny and hilarious, and there is a sense that Boris can take a joke. He never struck us as someone who went to sleep crying into his pillow because we said he looked like the *"…unlikely love child of Donald Trump and Angela Merkel"*.

While that seems like a pretty simple joke at first, it actually works in several ways: firstly, one can almost imagine the cruel trick of genetics that could produce Boris; secondly, at a deeper level, it rather sums up Boris's political dilemma. He sways between Trumpian populism and Merkelian centrism, never quite settling in one place or the other. As time went on, the joke gained new elements, particularly after Trump became President: it was so apparent that he and Merkel absolutely, viscerally, personally and politically hated each other, that the joke just got funnier and more ridiculous. It's funny how some jokes can run and run ("Thatcher jokes") where some, funny though they may be, have a very short shelf life indeed ("Truss jokes").

While writing this book, we've occasionally had to resort to Wikipedia to remind ourselves what a particular line we wrote was about. Some news stories aren't that memorable, we guess. Or we're just getting old and forgetting stuff. This is very possible. Tim's developed a very worrying symptom: He likes Werther's Originals. There, we've said it. He's self-identifying as an old git.

That's the thing about reality. You can't just pretend it isn't there or doesn't matter. Unless you're a theoretical physicist in which case these two assumptions are a prerequisite, and unless, of course, your name is Dementia J Trump.

Let's return to his 2020 election defeat and put Trump's tiny hands under the satirical microscope. Maybe we'll spot his alien blood.

Chapter Twenty-Four

Winners and Losers: whining as political art form.

2020-21

"The greatest test of courage on earth is to bear defeat without losing heart"

(Robert Green Ingersoll)

"No. I have to see. Look you – I have to see. No, I'm not going to just say 'yes.' I'm not going to say 'no.' And I didn't last time, either," (

Donald Trump on losing the 2020 election)

"I'll win this race fair and square, even if I have to cheat to do it.

(Dick Dastardly, Wacky Races)

	Popular vote	*%*	*Electoral College*
Trump/Pence	74,223,975	46.8	232
Biden/Harris	81,223,501	51.3	306

It's November 2020. Trump loses. Definitely. He'd said he definitely wouldn't, couldn't lose and as with most of what Trump says, it is utter and complete bollocks. In his words, not merely has he not lost, the election has been stolen from him, from America, and given to "sleepy Joe Biden", which makes it so much worse (or better, as one of the most delicious instances of schadenfreude ever, if you are so minded).

And as usual, it doesn't stop lots of people believing him: that he hasn't lost, that the election was stolen, and that Biden isn't the legitimate president. This is all fairly predictable but what is uncertain is exactly how far Trump and his MAGA cult will go. As it turns out, it is further than anyone had really predicted: they take the cherished American political tradition of the smooth handover of power and tell it to go stuff itself. Loudly and often.

To go along with Trump's usual stream of nonsensical bluster there develop several lines of attack from an increasingly embattled and random White House. First there is a legal route, or perhaps "legal" is a more accurate description. It is led by Rudi Guiliani and a ragtag of various "lawyers" who unlike most of their fellows haven't point blank refused to have anything to do with Trump's deranged flights of electoral fancy. This starts very badly after Giuliani & Co call a press conference in the hotly-contested city of Philadelphia. The assembled press are told it is "at the Four Seasons" but it turns out it wasn't the well-known hotel, but outside a gardening business with the same name, opposite a sex shop.

You couldn't make it up, So Donald did.

Reasons why Trump thinks he's won (reality):

He's got more votes than Biden (he hasn't)

> *He got more votes than he did last time, and he won then.* (True, but irrelevant.)

> *He'd lost so much of his term to Covid and various "witch hunts" he deserves a second term.* (He's lucky not to be moving from the White House directly to the Big House)

> *He can't have lost to Biden because Biden is a loser* (linguistically logical but utter tosh)

> *There was widespread electoral fraud, largely carried out by people who don't like him.* (There's clearly a long list of possible suspects here, not limited to the living. Very-definitely dead Venezuelan President Hugo Chavez is accused by Sidney Powell, one of Trump's legal team, of tampering with voting machines from beyond the grave.)

(Note to self: pitch remake of A Christmas Carol where Trump is haunted by the ghosts of Hugo Chavez, Richard Nixon and John McCain and completely fails to be redeemed in any way at all. Tiny Tim is forcibly deported and dies.)

Trump's utter refusal to concede defeat and his "legal team's" ever more bizarre conspiracy theories serve to radicalise the MAGA faithful and their anger begins to focus on one particular date: January 6th. This is the day when Congress will formally receive and accept the results of the election, under the chairmanship of Vice-President Mike Pence. Trump begins a social media campaign to encourage people to believe that Pence has some kind of leeway to refuse to accept the results presented to him. He absolutely has nothing of the kind, but as we've said many times, the truth is a moving target for Trump at best and of absolutely no consequence whatsoever at worst.

"If Mike Pence does the right thing, we win the election. All he has to do, all this is, this is from the number one, or certainly one of the top, Constitutional lawyers in our country. He has the absolute right to do it.*

*no, no he doesn't. And they aren't the "top constitutional lawyers" either. *Trailer Park Ambulance Chasers* is probably a better description, while also sounding like the kind of American TV series that Channel 5 show in the Uk because it's all they can afford, bless them.

A demonstration/rally is organised to take place not far from the Capitol in Washington DC on January 6th 2021. Trump takes to Twitter (his final flourish before his account is suspended) to promote the event:

Big protest in D.C. on January 6th. Be there, will be wild!

As it turns out, this is a rare understatement of reality by Donald's standards.

The large crowd at the rally are systematically inflamed by speaker after speaker, concluding with El Presidente himself, who gives a pretty unambiguous message to an increasingly angry crowd:

We want to go back and we want to get this right because we're going to have somebody in there that should not be in there and our country will be destroyed and we're not going to stand for that.

Because you'll never take back our country with weakness. You have to show strength and you have to be strong.

What happens next is – well, you know what it is, because it plays out on global television, first live, then goes on to be endlessly replayed and analysed for months afterwards. What we see seems almost impossibly strange at times, an armed mob trying to overthrow a democratically elected government and threatening the outgoing Vice President with the gallows. It's the best thing on telly by a country mile. Reality TV has finally gone feral and invaded the real world. People die, policemen and one of his own supporters, because of Trump's lies and if you ever need an example of why the truth matters there's a perfect one right here.

We do, however find one thing about the attack on the Capitol endlessly entertaining:

Just in front of the Capitol steps is a…. hotdog stand. It stays there throughout the attack on the Capitol and afterwards. Hungry business, insurrection. Assuming it isn't a cover for selling tear gas canisters and masks, that is.

The insurrection doesn't succeed, thank goodness. Congress, including many but not all Republicans, refuse to stand down and the election is certified in the early hours of January 7th. Fourteen days later Joe Biden is sworn in as the 46th President. Trump, like the brattish toddler he is, refuses to attend the ceremony and slinks off back to his Florida White House, Made-of-Lego, or whatever he calls it. The world sighs with relief. The nightmare is over, right? Trump will go back to what he does best: pretending to be rich and playing golf.

Everything can go back to normal. Not that anyone knows what that is anymore.

We swing our focus back to UK politics in 2022, to see if it's any less crazy than America's. We can but hope.

Chapter Twenty-Five

A short, sad story about a Truss with no support.

September-October 2022

"I am determined to deliver…" (Lis Truss, acceptance speech as PM. September 2022.)

"…I cannot deliver…" (Lis Truss, resignation speech, October 2022.)

"Stand and deliver" (Adam and the Ants, 1981.)

Lis Truss is probably destined to join the litany of embarrassing own goals and live TV foul-ups as little more than a future TV quiz question. She lasts as Prime Minister for 50 days in the Autumn of 2022, setting an unenviable record in the process. It isn't, however, a quiet 50 days. Rory asks us to find a pithy way of summarising it, see later in this chapter for the full salad leaf lowdown:

Queen dies after choking on lettuce. PM sunk by an iceberg.

Ok, yes, pithiness wins out over total accuracy there, so I guess we'll have to consider it at greater length.

Within days of the beginning of the "Truss era", Queen Elizabeth II dies: the UK loses its longest reigning Monarch, not unexpectedly but nonetheless a shock, especially given that no-one under the age of 75 has experienced the death of a monarch, or the Coronation of a new one. As it happens, we're driving to Cornwall from our home in Durham. We leave home as Elizabethans and arrive as a right pair of Charlies. Or something like that. Truss becomes the first PM to be in power at the death of a monarch since Winston Churchill, making them deeply unlikely bedfellows in yet another answer to a future quiz question. The Queen's final public appearance had been to welcome Liz Truss as Prime Minister at Balmoral. Within 48 hours, she is dead. Unfortunate timing. Indeed, accident-prone is probably the kindest way to describe the Truss premiership.

Not content with disposing of the Queen, Truss and Chancellor Kwasi Karteng seem keen to kill the economy too. He presents a 'mini budget' in the House of Commons on 29th September. Mini it may be but cautious it is not: it cuts the basic rate of income tax, abolishes the upper 45% rate and cancels a planned rise in corporation tax. It is shockingly radical. Or economically illiterate, depending on your point of view. The financial markets definitely belong to the latter camp and the stock exchange goes into freefall. By the end of the following day, the pound reaches its lowest level against the dollar ever. *Ever.* Generally, the financial world's response is a deafening slow handclap, with occasional boos.

It emerges that the Chancellor had not asked the Office of Budget Responsibility (OBR) to provide forecasts of the Budget's likely effects. He can only have done this because:

- He forgot.
- He knew if he did ask them, he wouldn't like the answer.
- He's an idiot.
- Truss told him not to and she's an idiot.
- Blame Boris. Why not?

The Daily Star (credit where it's due!) has set up a webcam showing an iceberg lettuce and a photo of Truss as PM, proposing that the lettuce will last longer than Lis. Ouch. They aren't wrong, either. By the time Truss resigns on 22nd October, the lettuce will still be jolly nice in a club sandwich and hasn't yet reached the final resting place of all icebergs – in one of those little bags of "salad" you get with an Indian takeaway.

So, it's all over, 50 days of financial ineptitude, regicide and flappy performances in the Commons. Whatever and whoever comes next has to be better, right?

At the time of writing, having left office and lost her seat in the 2024 Tory bloodbath, Ms Truss seems to have rather lost it. She's been pictured wearing MAGA hats, and has declared her love for Trump (eww). She wrote a book called "Ten Years to Save the West" – which argues, we assume, that the key thing is to keep her and her ilk far, far away from the levers of power in that decade. She also found some solicitors with a sense of humour and got them to write a letter to Kier Starmer telling him to stop saying that she crashed the economy. Kier's response is not recorded, although presumably Rachel Reeves pointed out that crashing the economy was her job.

So, my lords, ladies and gentlemen, we present Lis Truss, blink or you'll miss her as Prime Minister and the world's first self-satirising politician.

Appropriately, this is the shortest chapter in the book.

Ha.

Ha.

HA.

Chapter Twenty-Six

What is it good for? *Absolut*-ly Nothing.

2021-25

"Russia is seeking peace" (Vladimir Putin)

"I don't think that word means what you think it means." (The Princess Bride)

We're all about sequels these days and Big Bad Vlad the Invader isn't going to be left out. Russia had annexed the Crimea, legally part of Ukraine, in 2014 and for all that a treaty was signed between the two countries confirming Ukraine's right to exist, conflict between Kyiv and Russian-backed separatists grumbled on ever since.

Putin had absolutely no intention of sticking to the treaty and for him, the Crimea merely represented a jumping-off point for future territorial gains. Publicly he moaned on and on about the Russian-speaking Donbas region in the east of Ukraine being "historically" part of Russia, but what he was really worried about was a government in Kyiv that was looking West rather than East, towards membership of the EU, and ultimately of NATO.

Basically, Ukraine wants some new friends with deep pockets and a broad-based and frequently enthusiastic animosity towards Russia, and who could blame them?

That Ukraine government had been elected in 2019, under the presidency of one of modern history's more unlikely figures: Volodymyr Zelenskyy. Unlikely because he was young (41 when he took power) but really *very* unlikely because before standing for office he'd been the star of a TV Comedy Show called *"Servant of the People"* in which he'd played…wait for it…a fictional Ukrainian President. We were going to say you literally couldn't make it up but actually someone did, so we won't.

Rory's political ambitions have never stretched beyond imitating Prime Ministers and Presidents, but he is nonetheless incredibly passionate about politics. Indeed, you'd be hard pushed to find a political satirist, performer or writer, who doesn't care deeply about Politics and society. The point of satire isn't simply to throw rocks. Here's a thought experiment: if we had a government that was honest, competent, planned and implemented policies carefully, listened to opposing voices calmly, and governed fairly and openly for the whole population, would we need satire? I wonder.

Fortunately I don't think there ever has been a government that fulfils all those criteria. Kipling, before he got into baking, almost got it right.

> *If you can keep your majority when all about you*
>
> *Are losing theirs and blaming it on you,*
>
> *If you can trust yourself when Jon Snow doubts you,*
>
> *But make allowance for Boris being on Newsnight too;*
>
> *If you can bait and not be tired by baiting,*

Or being lied about, double down on lies,

Or being taxes, give way to tax evading,

And yet don't look too good, nor talk to spies..

Etc, etc You get the idea.

Satire is just one of the implements with which we question those we elect. Having said that, it's been interesting to note just how effective a leader, and a *war* leader Zelenskyy has been. Did anything in his past prepare him? Perhaps it's that in both phases of his life, he did something that reflected his passion for his society, and for good government. That's probably another book. (Finish THIS one. Ed.)

Right, yes. Back to Vlad's Bad Lads. Ukraine point blank refuse to back down on its EU and NATO membership ambitions. After months of *will he/won't he/of course he bloody will* over a possible invasion of Ukraine, Putin finally (and to no-one's surprise) pulls the trigger on 24th February 2022 on what he terms a "special police action", which is a bit like calling the World Cup "a bit of a kick about". It's quickly apparent that Russia's plan is simple: get to Kyiv really quickly, capture or kill Zelenskyy and his government and install a Russian puppet regime in its place.

It fails. Spectacularly. The Ukrainians had been planning for an invasion too and having allowed the Russian advance towards Kyiv, sneak in behind the Russian spearhead and cut its supply lines so the Russian troops quickly run out of food, oil and ammunition. Probably hope and vodka, too.

Since then there's been wall-to-wall media coverage of the war in all it's heartbreaking horror and you're probably, and understandably, worn down by it. With that in mind, here's our alternative timeline of some of the stories that you may have missed.

2021

December — First Putin Clone born. National Holiday in Russia (only for oligarchs).

After ever more stringent sanctions are imposed by the international community, the Ruble collapses. Attempts to estimate its new value can only be achieved using the Large Hadron Collider in Switzerland, which by a spooky coincidence is where the Oligarchs are rapidly moving all their money.

2022

February — Russia launches "special police action" in Ukraine. Putin says it could all have been avoided if Ukraine had brought back the lawnmower when they said they would.

Russia's thrust towards Kyiv grinds to a halt after Ukrainian forces sneak in behind them and cut their supply lines, depriving them of ammunition, food, fuel, vodka and hope. Russian agents planted in the city fail to participate in the action after their knock-off Soviet-era Mickey Mouse alarm clocks fail to go off.

The first Ukrainian hero of the war emerges as border guard Roman Hybrov tells the Russian warship to "go f*ck yourself" in response to a demand to surrender. Nice one.

March   Russian forces begin to occupy Russian-speaking areas in the east of Ukraine.

South Yorkshire appears to annex Bradford, in a copycat move, but it turns out it just wanted a curry.

April   Stalemate develops after Ukrainian counteroffensive. International community imposes wide-ranging sanctions on Russia, in particular attacking people known to be close to one of the Putins.

Putin said to be furious with Army's failure to meet any of their strategic goals and even more cross with Ukraine as Russia's lawnmower is now on eBay.

Numbers of Russian generals who've fallen out of high windows for no reason: 2.

May	Second Putin clone born. First Clone fully grown and ready to be unconvincing in visit to frontline troops.
	Population of all NATO countries wish someone would clone Zelenskyy to replace the shower of shite running their countries.
	May Day parade in Red Square consists of 27 Zil Limousines, a Putin clone, Donald Trump JR, Dwayne "the Rock" Johnson and an inflatable tank from Aldi.
	Ukraine win Eurovision and for once no-one actually minds about all the political voting. Liverpool offers to host the following year's event for Ukraine. Russia submits a counter-offer to host in Vladivostok, offering special free one-way ticket deals for all Ukrainian citizens who want to attend.
June	Russia strikes deal with China to supply missiles and military vehicles but when they arrive they're much smaller than they looked in the picture. Chinese ambassador falls out of window, but is discovered to be an android.
	Penny Mordaunt spotted wielding giant sword on battlefield close to the Russian border.
July	Stalemate. Numbers of defenestrated Generals: 5.
August	Major Ukrainian counteroffensive pushes back Russian forces in the Donbas. Google announces

that "where the hell is the Donbas" is most-searched term of the year.

Jeff Bezos buys Russia's lawnmower from ebay for the lolz, outbidding a user called vladKrem666 at the last second.

Third Putin clone produced after first one trips and falls out of a window. Second clone suspected of pushing him.

September — Second stalemate. NATO supplies Ukraine with armed attack drones: special regiment of fifteen year-olds formed to fly them.

Russia's lawnmower blasted into space on a Blue Horizon rocket and now orbiting Mars.

October — For Halloween, Russia holds solemn ceremony in which the names off all Russian soldiers killed so far are read out. Ceremony originally planned to be three hours long but lasts until March and is out of date three seconds after it finishes. Polls show that Zelenskyy is now more popular than pretty much anyone, even Global pop icon Taylor Swift and the Pope. Leaked documents show Rishi Sunak asked Nicola Sturgeon to consider invading Northumberland to increase his popularity. Plan scrapped after it's discovered that no-one south of Manchester either knows where Northumberland is, or thinks it's part of Scotland already.

November — Italian Prime Minister Giorgia Meloni is tricked by a pair of Russian pranksters posing as African leaders into recording an interview in which she says there's "a lot of fatigue" about the war. The EU council issue a statement saying they're pretty tired of her too.

Battlefield stalemate leads Ukraine to increasingly use drones to carry out attacks deep into Russian territory. One of the attacks on Moscow damages buildings and destroys the tank in which Putin clones four and five are being grown.

Pope accuses the Patriarch of Russian Orthodox Church of being "a whiny little bitch", but this is revealed to be just wishful thinking.

December — Complete failure to have a Christmas ceasefire as the two sides can't even agree when Christmas is. Santa Claus puts them both on the naughty list but secretly slips presents to Zelenskyy as he didn't start the fight.

Replacement Putin Clones four, five and six purchased from the Moscow branch of Lidl on a BOGOF offer. It emerges later that one of them is actually a clone of Gregg Wallace, and *no-one* wants that.

2023

January — Putin Clones form boy band called "Получите это, украинские ублюдки" (Take That you Ukrainian Bastards) and have Russia-wide hit with their debut single "Set Everything on Fire".

Denmark delivers 19 F16 aircraft to Ukraine, but the lack of experienced Ukrainian Lego builders renders them useless.

March — Putin signs a law making spreading false information about the war illegal and is immediately arrested by Clone Five.

Clone Five dies in 'abseiling accident' after forgetting to use a rope.

Germany and France both agree to send massive humanitarian and military aid to Ukraine. France also sends the crack Farmer "Road Block" Battalion armed with 200,000 dead sheep to piss off the Russians. Sweden announces a 7bn euro aid package, but admit they will charge another 1bn euros to deliver it.

On 29th February, Ukraine officially asks NATO to marry it. NATO is flattered but admits it is already in an abusive relationship with Switzerland.

June — Russia claims to have recaptured the Ukrainian village of Robotyne, but Ukrainian forces insist the fog there is still all theirs.

UK defence Secretary Grant Shapps promises 10000 drones during a visit to Kyiv but admits the UK will be waiting until they are on a Lightning Deal.

Ukrainian and anti-Putin Russian forces begin major incursion into Russian territory. Putin Clone Five turns out not to be dead after all and is seen driving a tank, waving an LGBTQ flag.

September — Ukraine offers formal thanks to vigilante hacker group "One Fist" for numerous cyberattacks on Russian infrastructure. It is believed that following one of these hacks, the Putin cloning facility is now only able to produce Gregg Wallaces.

Russia claim to have shot down five Ukrainian weather balloons but it's revealed that they were actually UFOs and that Russia is now also at war with Proxima Centauri 5. Boris Johnson clones, led by the original, are formed into special Space Force and carry out a suicide bombing of the sun. Celebrations ring out across the planet.

November — The UK government accuses China of supplying lethal aid to Russia and lethal electrical goods to everyone else.

Ukraine embarrassed after footage of a Russian plane being shot down turns out to actually be from a videogame. Activision win game industry award for "Best Viral Marketing Campaign" for their *Call of Duty: Fueled by Vodka* game.

2024

January The count of defenestrated generals reaches fifty: Moscow window cleaners go on strike demanding danger money.

Cloning facility able to produce Putins again, after a brief hiccup in which three Wiliam Hagues, a Lenin and a Jeff Bezos were accidentally produced and immediately destroyed, especially the Lenin.

President Zelenskyy reacts to UK election and says he's "relieved he'll never have to meet Grant Shapps again".

March Major Ukrainian incursion into Russia's Kursk Oblast. The notorious Wagner Group of mercenaries is deployed by Russia to repel the invasion, armed with a newly-weaponised version of *Götterdämmerung*.

Russia claim to have captured the village of New York* in eastern Ukraine. Rudi Giuliani offers to act as Mayor. *(*it really exists. We don't make everything up, you know.)*

Russia denies reports that no-one knows which one the real Putin is anymore, in a statement made by someone who no-one is sure is Putin.

July	Claims that the Democrats approached Russia regarding the possibility of making a clone of Barack Obama are rubbished after it's pointed out that Trump appears to think he's running against him anyway.
September	Russian forces capture the Ukrainian villages of Verkhnokamianske and Miasozharivka, thus registering the highest *Scrabble* score of the war to date.
	100 Ukrainian drones attack targets across Russia, who claim to have shot down 110 of them.*
	this is actually true. Sometimes reality's just funny.
November	Following his election victory, Trump calls Putin and advises restraint in Ukraine. Russia unable to confirm that the call happened as they're not sure which of the Putins he talked to. Neither is Trump.
	North Korean forces aiding Russia come under fire from Ukrainian forces for the first time but say it's still better than being at home.
December	Trump meets Zelenskyy at the ceremony to mark the opening of the refurbished Notre Dame Cathedral in Paris, where Zelenskyy hands out copies of a list of 40,000 buildings in Ukraine which also need to be rebuilt.
	...and on it goes, which is probably the only prediction that feels safe.

Chapter Twenty-Seven

Party politics, and other bloodsports.

2022-23

"Uneasy lies the head that wears a crown."

The King in Henry IV, Part 2

"I'm a schizophrenic narcissist. I hear voices but they're all me and they make a lot of sense."*

*(if the internal dialogue of some cabinet ministers was honest)

There's a centuries-old tradition in the UK of various kinds of mass-participant football-precursor games traditionally played on high days and holidays. They often involve hundreds of players all fighting over a ball or similar object on some huge field or around the streets of a town. Injuries and even deaths were once common. A few still survive, such as the *Ba* in Kirkwall on Orkney but the most telling modern equivalent is a Conservative Party Leadership Contest, which in the last decade occurred an unprecedented four times and featured betrayals, backstabbing and back-street fights over the rules. It also produced four Prime Ministers without an initial Electoral mandate, although both Johnson and May subsequently gained one, we have to hope largely out of shame.

Kick-off for the latest fixture happens swiftly after Lis Truss accepts the inevitable and resigns. The only candidate to replace her is the man she'd beaten to win the leadership mere weeks previously: Rishi Sunak. He triumphs after serial contestant Penny Mordaunt fails to get enough support from MPs to be on the ballot. Rishi had been Chancellor in the last Johnson cabinet and his resignation had been one of the key moments which led to Boris' resignation. Some cynical commentators (Tim) suggested that Rishi had been playing a long game all along: seeing an economy about to tank, he resigned and let the next budget be someone else's problem. Kwasi Karteng duly obliged with a budget best described as "completely incompetent". See the previous chapter for longer-form insults about it.

On 24th October 2022, Rishi Sunak becomes the first British Asian to hold the office of Prime Minister. An interesting sidenote: Lis Truss was the shortest serving PM, and the man who succeeds her is, at 5'7", simply the shortest. Funny old world.

It also means that the Tories have provided the first, second and third female Prime Ministers and, after the 2024 election debacle (spoilers), the first immigrant party Leader in Kemi Badenoch. Labour, meanwhile, seem to only trust white men to be its leader. The nearest they've ever got to diversity was the occasional Scot or someone not from Islington. It's not really a criticism as such, but you'd just expect, and perhaps hope that it would be the other way round, wouldn't you?

Perhaps the real reason the Tories choose Rishi is that it doesn't matter as they simply know they are going to lose the next election anyway. Despite its mercifully brief duration, the Truss premiership has been so damagingly, cringingly, even-worse-than-Boris awful, that the polls are giving Tory backbenchers post-traumatic flashbacks to 1997 and sending them scurrying to update their CVs or to give that Oxford chum who runs a hedge fund a quick call. In that light, you can understand why candidates aren't queuing up to captain HMS Tory Electoral Collapse.

Rishi's real political asset is his economic nous – he'd designed and implemented the furlough scheme which had (at eye-watering cost) kept the economy on life-support during COVID. One of his first actions as Prime Minister is to cancel most of the provisions of Kwasi's hari-kari mini-budget. None of this makes him remotely popular with the electorate, however: polls in November and December show Labour with a lead of upwards of 20 points. The "Rishi effect" turns out to be as disappointing as that cheap Chinese Christmas Tree you ordered at 3am which is a foot high and made of glittery flocked asbestos. It is increasingly evident that the public are simply sick to death of the Tories being in power and will kick them into the long grass at the first opportunity. The Tories themselves seem tired of the whole charade too. Fourteen years is a long time for everything to be your fault. It's possible that the electorate are also pretty ashamed of themselves and have made it their New Year's Resolution to stop voting Tory, for God's sake.

Before the inevitable end of Tory rule, we're about to experience something that no-one under the age of 80 can remember: a warm dry summer (joke) plus the Coronation of a new monarch. Prince Charles, having waited, and waited, and waited to become King, will finally ascend to the throne. He chooses Charles III as his regnal name, presumably hoping for a better outlook than the two previous King Charles' had: beheading and dying of an apoplectic fit, though the latter seems possible every time Prince Andrew appears in public or speaks to anyone.

The Coronation is a spectacle of British Pomp and Circumstance, and very splendid in a Gosh-I-do-like-this-new-season-of-*The-Crown* sort of way. Any hope the Tories have that a sudden fit of regally-fired patriotism might swing the electorate back in their direction prove to be utter fantasy, although the Coronation service does produce an unlikely breakout star: ex-Defence Minister and Tory leadership candidate Penny Mordaunt. She had run in the leadership election that Liz Truss won and been given the entirely powerless *ceremonial* position of Lord President of the Council as a reward, or more likely a punishment. No, we hadn't heard of it either – but it means she takes a front and centre ceremonial role in the coronation: carrying the massive seventeenth century Sword of State into the abbey and exchanging it for the Jewelled Sword of Offering, and looking, as is acknowledged across the political spectrum and indeed the world, thoroughly badass while doing it. Lis Truss sat watching from somewhere distant in the pews. Ha. Ha. Haaaaa.

It doesn't stop Ms Mordaunt losing her Portsmouth seat in 2024, either. Perhaps if they'd let her keep the sword that might have helped, but probably not. A Tory carrying a big sword is still a Tory, albeit one you might not pick a fight with.

13: Penny Mordaunt preparing for her role in the Coronation and feeling superior to Lis Truss.

The first Conservative electoral test under Rishi comes in the local elections later in May 2023 and it is, not to put too fine a point on it, a massively entertaining bloodbath. The Tories lose over a thousand council seats, primarily to Labour but also to the Lib Dems, Reform and the Greens. It's the kind of result that at another time could have brought about a Prime Minister's downfall but there doesn't seem to be any point. It's now a question of when the life support will be turned off, not when or how a recovery can start. It is so over for the Tories, just not yet.

Dead Short Man Walking.

Chapter Twenty-Eight

Vote early and vote often.

2024

"Many forms of Government have been tried, and will be tried in this world of sin and woe. No one pretends that democracy is perfect or all-wise. Indeed it has been said that democracy is the worst form of Government except for all those other forms that have been tried from time to time…..' (Winston Churchill)

"If voting changed anything, they'd make it illegal." (Emma Goldman)

Like the Elgin Marbles, we stole Democracy from the Greeks. The difference is, they can have Democracy back. (Tim and Mary Fowler)

As 2024 dawns, it is hailed, by those who notice such things, as the year in which there will be more elections globally that year than ever before. Kudos to whoever fell down an internet rabbit hole over Christmas to work that out.

Here are some of the highlights from the list of 2024's Electoral bonanza:

- USA
- UK
- Bangladesh
- Taiwan
- Finland
- Pakistan

- Wakanda
- Belarus
- Iran
- Ireland
- South Korea
- Lilliput
- Chad
- France
- Narnia
- Russia
- Moldova
- Qatar
- Sri Lanka
- Kanye West *(by-election)*
- Iceland *(a special referendum to settle once and for all why Mum does go there)*
- Venus
- Mars
- Snickers
- Bounty.

Obviously, some of the entries in this list are ridiculous and their results a concocted fantasy. Can you spot which ones? If you said Russia and Belarus, score two points – and if you want a bar of chocolate now, you're welcome.

For political junkies (Tim and Rory both freely admit to this addiction), this is all clearly very exciting and a chance to write lots of jokes. We presume Brenda from Bristol isn't so keen ("Oh no, not another hundred!") but that can't be helped. She may be dead, anyway. If she isn't, 2024 will likely make her wish she is.

Despite this global votedemic, our focus is, perhaps unsurprisingly, going to be largely on the two elections on opposite sides of the Atlantic, but if you want to know more about the other 98, that's what Wikipedia is for, and you can write your own bloody jokes.

The UK election is first out of the gates, earlier than anyone expected. It has to take place by November 2024 and the assumption is that Rishi will hang on for as long as possible, in the forlorn hope that something will happen to endear his deeply unpopular government to a justifiably angry electorate. Quite what might have to happen to have that effect is a poser: probably nothing short of a surprisingly right wing Second Coming: "Blessed are the meek for they shall be really easy to deport" etc.

As it turns out, even Rishi knows in every fibre of his short being that this won't happen, and he calls a snap election for July 4th, presumably so he can get the crushing defeat over and done with and get back to the serious business of living off his wife's money. Presumably Theresa May would have called that a "boy job".

In 2019, Boris Johnson and Nigel Farage had agreed to a deal whereby UKIP (as Reform were called before the rebrand) candidates were to stand down in Tory marginals, where they might have taken vital votes away. This was one of the tactics that won Boris his improbable majority.

There's no deal to save Rishi this time and it's clear that even if they don't win any seats, Reform can contribute to something verging on an electoral wipeout for the Tories. It's also clear that both public and private polling reflect rapidly growing support for Reform, a fact that sends hundreds of Tory MPs into a panicked death-spiral/ job hunt.

At times, it feels hard to distinguish between the parties, as their main selling point seems to be "we're not THEM". Here's a handy rundown of the party manifestoes to make things clearer, probably.

CONSERVATIVE

NHS *Pretend to spend more. Even when we do actually spend more it makes no difference so what's the fecking point?*

ECONOMY *It's shit, and all our fault but you're not going to vote for us anyway, so who the hell cares? Rishi???*

DEFENCE *Use SAS to kill bloody Farage.*

UKRAINE *You can tell how important we think this is by the fact that we let Grant Shapps do it. A significant number of our MP's think "Ukraine" is either one of Jacob Rees-Mogg's children or a weather forecast.*

CLIMATE *Expand nuclear power station building programme which will take 40 years to come on stream. Still, there might be another Tory Government by then, right? Hmmm.*

LABOUR

NHS *Spend more, blame the Tories when it makes no difference.*

ECONOMY *Blame Tories. Will put a strong, confident Chancellor into No.11. Or failing that, Rachel Reeves. Borrow recklessly and raise taxes while trying really hard not to crash the economy. (via the Hindsightoscope, we didn't even think in our most fevered imaginings that "take away pensioners winter fuel allowance then go after the disabled" would actually be the policy).*

DEFENCE *Maintain world class armed forces but promise to never ever ever ever EVER use them. Blair's gone. Promise.*

UKRAINE *Agree with whoever we last spoke to about this. We completely support either President Zelenskyy, Joe Biden, Trump or one of the Putins.*

CLIMATE *Wishful thinking. Experiment with "Make Britain Greta Again" slogan. Indicate how serious we are about energy security by making sure Ed Miliband will be Energy Secretary. LOL.*

LIB DEMS

NHS *Run a really big jumble sale to raise funds. New "Go for a nice walk" treatments.*

ECONOMY *Entire population to benefit from very very very expensive public spending increases funded by taxing the rich but it doesn't matter because we're not going to win.*

DEFENCE *Free knitted body armour for all soldiers.*

UKRAINE *All we are saying, is give peace a chance. but if that doesn't work, fecked if we know.*

CLIMATE *We were green before it was cool. Bastards.*

REFORM

NHS *Ban all the immigrant Doctors and Nurses from treating all the immigrant patients.*

ECONOMY *Force unemployed to do all the jobs the immigrants we're going to chuck out used to do.*

Or

Sell the UK to Elon Musk. "You can't spell Musk without UK!"

DEFENCE *Invade France. Make Britanny British Again!*

UKRAINE *We support Russia in its attempts to reverse Ukrexit and see no contradiction in this position whatsoever.*

CLIMATE *Denial. Extinction Rebellion to be classified as terrorists. Background checks required before you can buy tomato soup, orange paint or superglue.*

GREEN

NHS *Accuse Lib Dems of stealing our "go for a nice walk" proposal.*

ECONOMY *Turn all football pitches into allotments. Relocate Bank of England, Stock Exchange and Treasury to Brighton and turn them into vegan café cooperatives.*

DEFENCE *Disband the Services. Turn tanks into planters for urban vegetable gardens. Erect hand-crafted 'Please Don't Invade Us' signs around the coast.*

UKRAINE *Peace talks to be held in Brighton, vegan snacks provided.*

CLIMATE *REPENT YE! REPENT YE! RECYCLE YE!*

THE FOUR CYCLISTS OF THE CLIMATE ARMAGEDDON ARE UPON US!

MONSTER RAVING LOONEY

NHS *A carefully thought out and properly funded root-and-branch reform of the service to make it fit to meet the challenges of the 21st Century.*

Free clown noses for all NHS managers

ECONOMY *Institute a fair and progressive tax system where everyone pays their fair share. Launch a Universal Basic Income to replace dehumanising benefit system.*

All tax evaders to be hit in face with custard pies.

DEFENCE *Reassess defence spending in the light of Britain's post Brexit standing in the world, while maintaining our commitment to NATO and UN peacekeeping forces. Free marmite for all sailors!*

UKRAINE *Support Ukraine financially and humanitarily while urging compromise and peace talks. Avoid escalatory actions. Maintain constructive back-channel contacts with Moscow.*

Propose peace talks to be held in hot air balloon floating three hundred feet over North Pole with Santa as mediator.

CLIMATE *Use government intervention to make both small and large scale green energy projects appealing. Commission fast-track development of new generation of Type IV passively cooled, safe Nuclear plants, thereby prioritising energy security in a post-oil world.*

Personal wind turbine hats for all!

There, I bet you wish you'd had that before the election, don't you?

It's a peculiarly listless campaign. The electorate clearly hate the Tories and want shot of them, but this doesn't seem to translate into a burning enthusiasm for Keir Starmer's Labour, who feel like the least-worst-best-option.

It feels very different to the last time Labour stood on the verge of power in 1997 when there was a palpable sense that the shadow cabinet was a highly competent government-in-waiting. It doesn't help that Keir, nice chap as I'm sure he is, no doubt kind to dogs and children, is as inspiring as a week-old bucket of wet cement.

We realise that could look like we're saying that he is particularly appealing to bricklayers, but no, they probably don't like him either. Kier's great and lasting appeal is that he isn't a Tory. That's it. And that's all he needs to win, and win BIG.

Turnout: 28,924,725 (59.8%, down 7.5%)

	Votes	*Vote Share*	*Seats*
Conservative	6,828,925	23.7% (down 19.9%)	121 (down 251)
Labour	9,708,716	33.7% (up 1.6%)	412 (up 211)
SNP	724,758	2.5% (down 1.4%)	9 (down 39)
Lib Dem	3,519,143	12.2% (up 0.7%)	72 (up 64)
Reform UK	4.117,610	14.3% (up 12.3%)	6 (up 6)
Green	1,944,501	6.7% (up 4%)	4 (up 3)

As expected, Labour win a landslide in terms of seats, gaining 211 seats while the Tories lose 251, leaving them with an embarrassing but survivable 121. Some polls had suggested that the Conservative vote could have collapsed like a cheap bouncy castle. Labour's landslide, meanwhile, has come with a smaller vote share than any of the three Blair victories *(ok Tim, get over it – Mary).*

The shocking/fascinating results are further down the ballot: the Lib Dems secure a record 72 seats on 12.1% of the votes, up 64, suggesting the electorate *may* have finally forgiven them for propping up the Cameron government in 2010. If you've forgotten about that, go back and read chapters one and two immediately. And pay attention this time. The shock is that Reform poll 14%, out of nowhere. This gives them five seats and in so doing achieves something extraordinary: it makes Nigel Farage a fan of Proportional Representation.

"It is my view that the outdated first past the post system is no longer fit for purpose."

He's right, of course, but it also highlights the centre-left orthodoxy's problem with PR: they love that it would mean more Green and Lib Dem MPs*: but ugh, what if people actually, you know, vote for someone we don't like, someone who's* **wrong** *about all those things we* **know** *we're* **right** *about?*

Idiots. Be careful what you wish for.

Sometimes comedy writes itself: in Scotland, the SNP are almost wiped out by Labour, representing a fall from the giddy McHeights of 2014 on a truly spectacular scale. Corruption, an obsession with a second Independence referendum that a majority of Scots said in poll after poll that they don't want and a series of publicity nightmares over their backing of a gender recognition act that is profoundly unpopular. It becomes all too clear that Scots prefer JK Rowling's stand on the issue to Nicola Sturgeon's, who's managed to become the Delores Umbridge of Scottish politics, appropriately enough. A second Indyref now seems about as likely as Scotland winning the World Cup (any of them).

As the school year ends shortly after the election it seems reasonable to imagine some end-of-year reports for the party leaders:

Westminster Commons Comprehensive School

Headmaster: Sir Anthony Charles Linton Blair Ba(Oxon), MA International Relations (Baghdad)(failed)

Keir Starmer

Kier tries hard and has served effectively, if not inspiringly, as Deputy Head boy and his campaign slogan of "You could do worse" seems to sum that up nicely.

His academic performance is good, if not inspiring. Economics continues to mystify him and nothing our Head of Economics, Mr Balls, can say seems to break through. The incident where he copied from his neighbour Rachel in a test is best glossed over, particularly as they both got the answer wrong.

In extra-curricular terms, Keir is involved in lots of societies and is a keen, if not inspiring team member in several sports. His position as reserve in the debate society is very secure, and his fellow team members often speak of his ability to have a glass of water ready when they really need one.

His recent elevation to Captain of the Westminster Cabinet First XI coincided with their worst season in school history and the setting of a new record for own goals scored.

Summary: Not inspiring. Must try harder. For God's sake. Please.

Rishi Sunak

Despite nominally serving as head boy until the end of the year, in all honesty it felt like he left the school some time ago. His letter requesting that he miss the School Remembrance Service as he had an interview with a leading merchant bank that day, has been framed and hangs on the staffroom wall in a place of honour.

While his increasing absence from the school has been frustrating, we must all remember how well he stepped up after the expulsion of Elizabeth Truss following the "incident" and the unfortunate passing of beloved school corgi, Queenie.

We're sure Rishi will do very well and ask him to remember us when he's looking to avoid tax by making massive charitable donations, particularly if Kier succeeds in his campaign to charge VAT on school fees, the Quisling berk.

Summary: 01-65-43, account number 0034761865. Thanks.

Ed Davey

Sorry, Headmaster. I can't bring him to mind.

(Headmaster's note: no problem. Neither can anyone else.)

Summary: Who?

Carla Denyer & Adrian Ramsey

As Joint Presidents and sole members of the school branch of Extinction Rebellion, Carla and Adrian continue to offer a distinctive contribution to school life, albeit that the art department paint cupboard now has to be kept locked at all times. Their insistence on being referred to jointly as they/them has caused great confusion at times.

Negotiations to transfer them to a school in Brighton are underway and we feel this will be a good thing for all concerned, even if we have to superglue them on to the bloody train.

Summary: could try less hard and contribute much less to class, please.

Nigel Farage

Despite leaving in 1998 Nigel continues to attend school for reasons known only to himself. He has a collection of leavers' hoodies unparalleled in school history. Although having now studied Economics, History and Geography for almost three decades, he still seems to have little or no grasp of any of the subjects. It doesn't help that he refuses to attend classes taught by Mr Lewandanski or Ms Sidhu.

Summary: Leave. Please. And yes, we get the irony of that.

As the electoral juggernaut of 2024 rumbles on and on, a remarkable global trend becomes dramatically apparent (and for once it isn't some insane craze like eating golf balls started by bloody TikTok): everywhere, literally everywhere with a genuinely democratic election, parties in power lose vote share, and many are ousted from government. The reason seems clear: the world's economy is in dire straits, with inflation an inevitable consequence of the post-COVID boost in demand. Coupled with the huge amount of debt that has been incurred by governments worldwide, simply to get through the pandemic with a living, breathing economy, it's an imperfect storm. Nothing hits a population like inflation: we notice it because we see it every time we shop, or pay our gas bills, or fill the car with petrol. The kind of headline economic data that influences markets and investors, simply doesn't play if a six pack of toilet roll costs 50p more than it did 6 months ago, and you need a mortgage to fill your car up.

Across the EU, where centre-left parties had been in power for a decade and longer, their loss of vote share results in a dramatic swing to the right. The UK continues to be outlier with a swing to the left: albeit only because the right had been in power for so long:

> *It's just a jump to the left*
> *As Europe steps to the right*
> *Put your hands on your wallet*
> *You rein your costs in tight*
>
> *But it's those price rises*
> *That really drive you insane*
> *Let's do the 1930's Time Warp again*
> *Let's do the 1930's Time Warp again*

The swing towards populism in Europe rides a wave of anti-government feeling that has been rumbling away since COVID. People are angry and someone has to pay. This leads to some very divisive and unpleasant language being used to whip up that anger to an even greater level. Giorgia Meloni, who led the populist wave when she became Italian PM in 2022, repeatedly says that her goal is "to defend God, Fatherland and Family", which is straight out of the 1930's right-wing playbook. It's interesting that language like this finds an audience at the exact time when the generation that lived through 1930-1945 are almost entirely no longer around to sound a warning voice.

Inevitably, social media helps to disseminate these dangerous ideas, literally at the speed of light. I suppose we must be forever grateful that Instagram wasn't around in the 1930s:

@Goebbels

Lit mega turnout to hear @dasfuhrerdude speak at Nuremberg today. Sick. #einvolkeinreicheinfuhrer #Bolshevismsucks

Click here to buy your authentic Poland edition jackboots – only 500DM: www.triumphofthewill.de

Sound familiar? Of course it does, because there is someone who is doing and saying things very, very like that. And he is running for Fuhrer – sorry, President again. Gott in Himmel.

Chapter Twenty-Nine

The future's dark, the future's Orange.

2024

"To hell, allegiance! Vows, to the blackest devil!

Conscience and grace, to the profoundest pit!

I dare damnation. To this point I stand

That both the worlds I give to negligence.

Let come what comes, only I'll be revenged"

(Shakespeare, Hamlet, Act 4 Sc 5)

"I am your warrior. I am your justice. And for those who have been wronged and betrayed, I am your retribution."

(Donald J Trump, 'My Greatest Speeches', Act 45, Sc 279)

Stephen King's novel, and subsequent films, *'It'* concern an evil shape-shifting monster who returns to haunt generation after generation of innocent child victims. Why we feel the need for that to be the opening sentence in a chapter about Donald Trump's campaign in the 2024 presidential election we leave up to you. Safe to say that for many the result is yet another sequel in another long-running horror franchise: *A Nightmare on Pennsylvania Avenue.*

It is clear from very early in the year that Trump will be the nominee, criminal convictions - all 34 of them - notwithstanding.

Trump's MAGA cult still has a sadistic choke-hold on the Republican party and there's no safe word. It is much less clear who he'll be running against: Joe Biden will be 82 on Inauguration Day 2025 and increasingly looks and sounds uncertain and forgetful. It isn't clear when he faces the press whether he is going to make a speech or hand round Werthers Originals to everyone. It doesn't help that Trump's numerous slips, dissociations and downright crazy stuff he says almost constantly are reported at a much lower pitch than Biden's. It all comes to a peak in the first TV Debate where Biden's performance is stumbling, and Trump by comparison simply looks stronger and smarter, extraordinary as that sounds.

Biden seems determined to stay, hanging on desperately to the idea that he had beaten Trump once – which no-one else could say - and can beat him again. Yes, and Tim played off a 4 handicap when he was 18, and now he'd basically just drive round in a golf cart digging holes with a four iron and 5-putting the greens while swearing a lot. It occurs to us that golf-obsessed Trump would like this metaphor and now we feel dirty and need to have a shower. Eww.

The debate in Democratic circles (largely behind closed doors) grumbles on until the summer, when Biden is finally convinced to step aside. The clinching meeting appears to be with 83-year-old Nancy Pelosi and one assumes that when someone older than you tells you you're too old, it hits home. The problem now is, with the election fewer than four months away, there simply isn't time to run a set of primary elections to elect a new candidate. The spotlight therefore falls on Kamala Harris, Biden's Vice-President, as being the only plausible candidate, despite the low approval ratings and low-profile she suffers from as VP.

It's also distinctly possible that other potential candidates such as Pete Buttigieg (Secretary of Transport under Biden); Governor of Michigan Gretchen Whitmer and Pennsylvania Governor Josh Shapiro feel that a Trump victory is likely whoever runs against him and that being the sacrificial lamb is a bad career move. Or bad movie: 'The Silence of the Sacrificial Lambs'. Of course, they can all run in the 2028 election.

Assuming there is one, that is. During the campaign, Trump tells a rally of the Christian Right that they have to make sure they vote this time, because if they elect him, they "won't need to vote again." It's hard to read that in anything other than a sinister, straight from the Hitlerian playbook, sort of way.

Trump's campaign is pretty much as expected, a "revenge tour" of rally after rally in whatever cavernous space is available (other than the inside of Donald Jr's skull, interestingly). He rails against old targets (Mexicans, the mainstream media & Barack Obama – who he occasionally seems to think he's running against) and new targets (all migrants, the Justice Department and the various special prosecutors and district attorneys who are rightly prosecuting him). Republican talking heads and pundits insist that Trump should be "taken seriously but not literally", which is pretty mind-bending if you think about it. Then, God help us, someone in the campaign teaches everyone the word "hyperbole" and suddenly it's all over the media. We strongly suspect that at least half those using it don't know when it means. And think it rhymes with 'Super Bowl'.

That's a good example of a joke that only works when written down.

When Trump was kicked off Twitter and Facebook after the 2020 election (and before his new BFF Elon Musk let him back) he founded his own microblogging site called Truth Social which was funny because almost everything he posted or reposted on it was an antisocial lie. LOL.

He makes wild promises about solving the Ukraine war "in a day" and imposing punishing tariffs on imports – without either he or his audience understanding that doing that will increase prices of imported goods. Presumably drug dealers and arseholes are particularly piqued about the likely huge increase in the price of BMWs and Maybachs.

As his running mate, he chooses J.D. Vance, a Senator from Ohio who has at one point called Trump "America's Hitler". Perhaps Trump took this as a compliment and it is the *reason* he picks Vance to be his VP.

He continues to use the language of autocracy and fascism, talking about "enemies of the people", demonising migrants by telling downright lies about them – most memorably and shockingly that Haitian immigrants in Ohio are eating pet cats and dogs. Challenged on his autocratic tendencies in a TV interview, he says that he will be "a dictator on day one", causing those of us brought up watching Mr Benn on children's television to wonder if he is going to be an astronaut on day 2, a knight in armour on day 3 and then a clown for the next four years.

And then, on July 13th…

…somebody shoots at him. At an open-air rally in Butler, Pennsylvania, Trump is nicked in the ear by a bullet or fragment of something a bullet hit – it's still not clear which - and is rushed from the stage by Secret Service while dripping blood and raising a defiant fist. This scene leads to a photo which improbably makes many people recall that ultimate icon of American bravery under fire: the raising of the flag on Iwo Jima during the Second World War:

Our first reaction is one probably shared by many: sodding liberals, can't even shoot straight. Then it becomes apparent that the shooter (himself shot and killed by a Secret Service that had incompetently let him get within line-of-sight shot of the candidate), was, to judge by his social media, a fully paid-up MAGA cultist. The WTAF nature of 2024 never fails to disappoint.

Who fired and why the shots were fired rapidly takes a distant second to the fact that Trump has "miraculously" survived. For a Presidential candidate happy to buy into the idea that he is destined to be President because God wants him to be, it is manna from heaven. For many, it's the defining moment that guarantees he'll win the election. Godammit.

It's an interesting and possibly terrifying thought experiment to speculate on what might have happened had Trump not survived. The consequences might have been considerably worse than the prospect of another Trump presidency. It's perhaps a little hyperbolic to suggest that America escaped a second civil war by an inch or two but the wrath of the heavily armed MAGA cult robbed of their figurehead is all too easy to imagine. We're talking

Tesco on the last Saturday before Christmas, with automatic weapons, body armour and pipe bombs.

To her credit, Vice-President Harris runs an energetic and positive campaign, promising that it is time to "go forward, not back" and presenting a clearly sane alternative to the increasingly unbalanced Trump. She selects Minnesota Governor Tim Walz as her running mate, a man who looks like he's walked straight out of The Waltons and who verges on the cuddly. If they win, Build-a-Bear will sell millions of Walz Bears.

Unfortunately, as it turns out, a positive, professional, modern campaign can't beat a sprawling dystopian nightmare led by a death-defying what-a-messiah in a straight fight.

In these troubled times, we're often drawn inexorably to Shakespeare and "*a tale, told by an idiot, full of sound and fury, signifying nothing*" from Macbeth seems a pretty good description of Trump's campaigning style.

But.

It.

Works.

As in 2016, much of the world stares on in shock as Trump not only wins the electoral college but also the popular vote, something he'd not achieved in either previous campaign, though it isn't the landslide he claims. Not that it matters.

	Popular vote	*%*	*Electoral College*
Trump/Vance	77,303,573	49.9	312
Harris/Walz	75,019,257	48.4	226

Dear God.

Despite polls which had consistently shown neck and neck races in vital swing states with leads within the margin of error, Trump wins handily in the electoral college and by a small but significant margin in the popular vote. Suddenly, all the Trump campaign noise about rigged elections and Democrat cheating stops. Whodathunkit?

Tim also feels particularly got at as he realises that every time there is someone called Tim on the Democratic ticket, Trump wins. FFS.

November 6th dawns and the world once again faces four years of a Trump presidency. Rory calls early that morning asking for material for various shows he's been asked to go on, which is a nice reminder that whatever else the next four years will bring, Trump is great to write jokes about. Every cloud and all that:

> *He's the convicted felon but we're the one getting the four year sentence.*
>
> *He'll get a State visit to England and a 'State o'that' visit to Scotland.*
>
> *Queen tells medium that she's "glad she's dead".*

Poor Melania. What has she got to look forward to? Another four years as Donald's third wife, and for the second time, the First Lady. And then being buried on a tacky golf course.

I can't work out if it was Trump's racism or misogyny that was the bigger vote-winner.

Melania may be able to get a divorce on grounds of infidelity as he's definitely about to screw Ukraine.

Movie sequels coming next year: Trump 2, World War 3 and Horsemen of the Apocalypse 4.

Dark? Yes. Trump's President again, why wouldn't it be dark?.

As we write, Trump's putting together his cabinet of curiosities – people are being proposed and then abandoned so rapidly due to their often-horrendous unsuitability, that the Secretary of State is probably Oscar the Grouch by now. What's even more alarming is the proposed attempt for MAGA to take over the civil service by putting political appointments into posts normally held by federal employees chosen on merit. Putting the fox in charge of the henhouse doesn't even come close. In 2016, we didn't really know what Trump would do in his four years but this time we've got what could loosely be called a plan, and it's a truly terrifying one: Project 2025. We've read it so you don't have to and here's our summary:

Holy shit.

It's a more comprehensive precis than you might imagine, as the 920-page document proposes, amongst other things, turning the USA into a Christian Nationalist state, and embedding "family values" into every level of government and state. It's not clear which family they mean but it's either the Waltons or the one in Texas Chainsaw Massacre.

So, another four years of Trump begins. If the last 12 years have taught us anything, prediction is a mug's game. We don't know what these years will bring, good, bad, indifferent. We only know one thing.

We'll write comedy about it.

Chapter Thirty

The end, for now.

2025

"Think'st thou that duty shall have dread to speak when power to flattery bows? To plainness honor's bound when majesty falls to folly."

Kent in *King Lear, Shakespeare* (1.1.164-167)

King Lear, it should be remembered. is a play about a foolish old man who divides his kingdom, goes mad, there's a storm and everybody dies. It's basically Shakespeare does Trump. We hope.

And that's where we stop.

What a deeply extraordinary twelve years it's been. If we could send a copy of this book back in time, no one would believe a bloody word.

Boris, Prime Minister, Donald Trump, President? No. Not a chance. A pandemic? What, like in **Outbreak**? *NAH. Trump AGAIN?? You're having a laugh.*

Well, actually, we hope *you* are having a laugh.

It's been a dozen years characterised by indecent amounts of voting: since 2012 there have been four general elections, three US Presidential elections, a referendum and twelve series of *I'm a Celebrity Voice of Britian's Got Strictly Big Brother Island*. There've been some interesting trends: Labour's failure to win election after election that they should have won, the Tories shamefacedly taking advantage of that and the Lib Dems' electoral journey from being a little bit loved in 2010 to being hated and ignored (2015-19) and then being loved again (2024), a little bit more. The Greens got lots of votes and until 2024, one seat. Nigel Farage kept coming back and back like a bad pfennig and finally got into Parliament just as all his Tory mates were leaving. He's now engaged in an uneasy love triangle with Trump and Elon Musk so God knows what he'll do next. Let's hope they don't breed.

Turnout in the UK elections varied, showing a steady fall over the period, seemingly hand in hand with a growing dissatisfaction with the whole idea of every vote mattering, or indeed that it could really change anything. It's important to acknowledge that just before our story opens, the UK had a referendum on Proportional Representation and not enough people worried about every vote counting to vote for a change to a system where that would happen. Nonetheless, however flawed our system may be, the fact remains that voting is the one way we can actually change things, and we should all vote, all the time, at every opportunity. It's certainly the case that older people tend to vote more than younger generations and this has a real effect on the policies that end up in manifestos: it's why you hear more about the triple lock on pensions and squabbles over planning permission and less about Student Loans or Green policies during election campaigns. Big upturns in young people voting have been forecast at every general election in the last 20 years but it's still to appear in a meaningful way. Taken together, all of this means that UK elections are often decided by people who think Squid Game is number 42 on the local Hong Kong Kitchen menu. Perhaps we should make it easier to vote, less trekking to your local primary school in the rain and more voting on an app, like *Love Island*:

"Are Keir and Rachel your favourite couple, or do you prefer Rishi and Penny? You decide who gets to move into the Downing Street Villa!"

Ian Stirling could anchor the Election night coverage. We'd watch. In fact, with Mary's addiction to reality television running at an all-time high, she'd be glued to the screen, downloading the app and keeping Tim up to date with who snogged who in the Hideaway/Ministry of Health office. Sorry, not sorry, Matt Hancock.

In Australia, it's a legal requirement to vote. In fact, it's one of only 23 countries with mandatory voting laws. (Tim would like to point out, particularly as 2025 is an Ashes year, that almost everyone in Australia is there *because* of a "legal requirement"). Failing to register to vote and go to the polls are breaches of the law applicable to all aged 18 years and above, potentially leading to a fine and possibly a court summons. What would Brenda from Bristol make of that? Is this a policy that aligns with democracy? Is Australia more democratic than the UK or is it just their natural smugness showing through? That's a matter for debate. Maybe we should put it to the vote.

Mary (who loves all things Australian) would like to apologize on Tim's behalf for most of that last paragraph because there isn't a cat in hell's chance of him doing it. In fact there's more chance of him apologizing to the cat.

Here's a handy (and at least partially accurate) graph to summarize all those UK elections:

Number of seats/jokes/fecks given

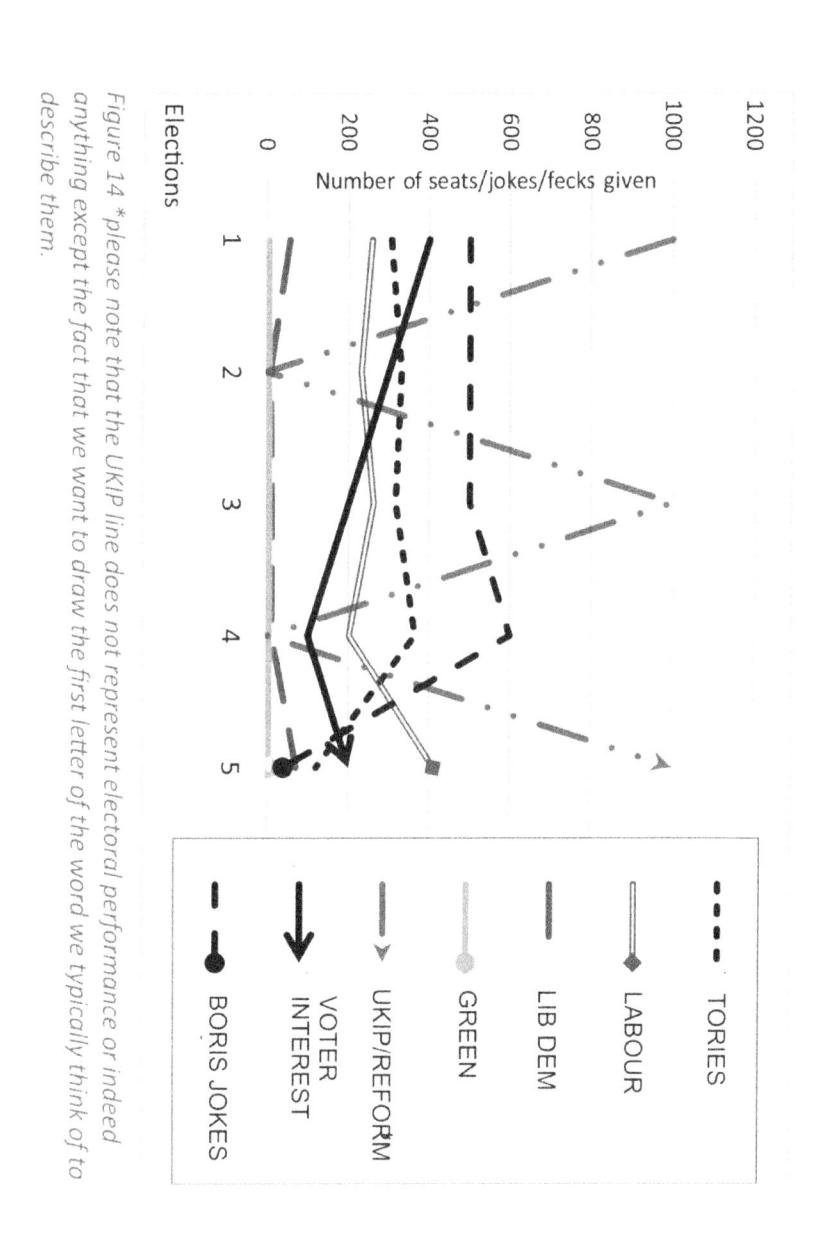

Elections

Legend:
- TORIES
- LABOUR
- LIB DEM
- GREEN
- UKIP/REFORM
- VOTER INTEREST
- BORIS JOKES

Figure 14 *please note that the UKIP line does not represent electoral performance or indeed anything except the fact that we want to draw the first letter of the word we typically think of to describe them.

That's all clear now, isn't it? Yes? Good.

We don't even need a graph to summarize the US elections, which have taken on a certain depressing rhythm:

OH SWEET JESUS IT'S TRUMP/NOT TRUMP/PLEASE GOD NO, IT'S TRUMP AGAIN.

Boom.

Writing satirical comedy is a task much like the archetypical painting of the Forth Road Bridge: almost by definition, it ends only when as a writer you choose to stop. There will always be new follies and new fools to satirise, a new rain of bad ideas and all too often, a drought of good ones and of good people to implement them. Injustice seems sadly endemic to all human societies and satire can be one of the tools we use to challenge it. It is, at its best, meeting fire with fire, meeting generalised rage with a comedic scalpel guided by controlled anger.

If you think you'd like to have a go at, here's our two (euro*) cents.

we have Irish passports and are intolerably smug about it.

How to do it? Use the very first skills you learned in your education: read, and write.

Read widely, read critically, read blogs, Twitter/X, Facebook, news websites, - or if you're feeling analogue - newspapers, books and magazines too. Read things you agree with passionately and read even more of the things that enrage you beyond words. Watch the news from as many sources as possible. Truth has always been a moving target, and in the 2020's it is more elusive than ever: learn to recognise it and only trust those sources who deserve it. We know who ours are but there's no point in telling you. You need to find your own. We will say one thing: if all the sources you follow say the same thing, you're living in an echo chamber and you need some new ones. We think we may very well have had more inspiration for material from reading the *Express* and the *Daily Mail* rather than the *Independent* because it takes us out of our echo chamber and introduces us to alternative points of view.

As a subset of read: listen, and watch. There's a lot of comedy about and in terms of its accessibility it's a golden age. The Netflix special has taken comedy out of the clubs and local theatres and on to phones, tablets and TVs across the world. Who makes you laugh? Why is it funny? How do those jokes work? There are always two elements here: writing and delivery. We've been fortunate to write for one of the best deliverers of a line there is but there are lots of good ones to watch and analyse.

Write: Write jokes. Lots of them. Awful ones, unbroadcastable ones (Tim has a password-protected note on his phone with these in it), ones you'd never tell your mother, ones your mother might tell and make you wish she hadn't – and if you do that, every now and then you'll write a good one. We got to the point where we unplugged our Alexa when we were trying jokes out on each other for fear the bad taste police would hammer down our front door and arrest us. You won't know where the line is until you've gone past it and can look back.

We also recommend drinking a lot of tea and always having biscuits to hand. Gin works for some people and takeaways are a nice reward after a long day at the joke factory. There's a reason there isn't a comedy writing diet book.

(Note: pitch comedy writing diet book. "You'll never have enough money to overeat.")

When you do write a joke that you think works, look at it, walk around it, get to know it. Why does it work? What *exactly* is the thing in it that's funny? What makes it yours? As with any writing, finding your own voice is an essential part of your journey – and when you find it, there are few more exhilarating experiences. We both treasure the moment when Rory told us there were "Tim and Mary" jokes, material that was uniquely "Us".

This book has, in some ways, been a process of developing that voice. We wanted to take all that (good!) material we'd written and turn it into an illustrative thread that could tell us something about the last twelve years, tell you something – and of course, to make you laugh.

Both Mary and Tim honed their craft in the early days of Twitter, when the 140 character limit was both a curse and a blessing, as it made *good* joke-writing challenging and a necessarily precise exercise. In fact, this book wouldn't exist without Twitter jokes: we met there and as chronicled in the introduction, Tim started writing for Rory after he had a joke go viral on Twitter. As a reward for making it to the end of the book, here's what that joke was:

> *The big bottle of gin I bought earlier was £22 after the budget but I'm still going to party like it's £19.99.*

See? Told you need to write a lot of bad jokes.

Think about who makes you laugh. It doesn't matter if it's a professional comedian, a family member or a mate. Finding your funny is about absorbing as much as possible of other peoples' funny too. We all need our heroes, and comedy is no exception. We're incredibly lucky that we get to write for one of ours. Rory's been making us laugh for decades before we ever penned a single joke for him. So it's important that this book ends like this:

Thank you, Rory, for letting our funny become part of yours.

MF & TF 2025.

Printed in Great Britain
by Amazon